**Jadesola James** loves summer thunderstorms, Barbara Cartland novels, long train rides, hot buttered toast, and copious amounts of cake and tea. She writes glamorous escapist tales designed to sweep you away. When she isn't writing, she's a university reference librarian. Her hobbies include collecting vintage romance paperbacks and fantasy shopping online for summer cottages in the north of England. Jadesola currently lives in Long Island, New York. Check out what she's up to at jadesolajames.com!

This is **Jadesola James**'s debut book for Mills & Boon Modern

We hope that you enjoy it!

And check out Jadesola's debut for Carina Press, *The Sweetest Charade*!

# REDEEMED BY HIS NEW YORK CINDERELLA

JADESOLA JAMES

MILLS & BOON

First published in Great Britain 2021
by Mills & Boon, an imprint of HarperCollins*Publishers* Ltd,
1 London Bridge Street, London, SE1 9GF

www.harpercollins.co.uk

HarperCollins*Publishers*
1st Floor, Watermarque Building,
Ringsend Road, Dublin 4, Ireland

Large Print edition 2022

Redeemed by His New York Cinderella © 2021 Jadesola James

ISBN: 978-0-263-29494-1

01/22

FALKIRK COUNCIL LIBRARIES

To Aunty B, who gifted me my first stack of Harlequin Presents so long ago.

I hope you love this one!

# CHAPTER ONE

LAURENCE JAMES STONE hadn't eaten alone in a hotel dining room in years.

He had no idea why he'd chosen to do so tonight. The Park Hotel's quiet elegance, shrouded in greenery on the north end of a mid-Manhattan street, possessed the sort of shabby opulence that was no longer favored by the rich and young. However, the food was sublime, the service impeccable—and in a manner of hours he would be hosting the biggest social event of the season in the Grand Ballroom.

His advertising firm, recently gone public, would be the talk of the evening. He and his business partner were so close to hitting the billion-dollar mark that he could taste it. That number had eluded him for years, and though his personal fortune was vast, this was different. He wanted to be able to *pay* himself that amount, created by his own hand.

This, in a way, was their debut.

Laurence had arrived and been ushered to the penthouse suite in plenty of time to rest and dress for the evening's festivities, after an eight-hour flight from Berlin, but his stomach had started growling thirty minutes after his arrival, even though he'd been offered a bewildering assortment of food on the flight.

He'd showered and thrown on a sweater and wool trousers, then taken the penthouse elevator down. He'd looked forward to this quiet meal. Perhaps it was because he'd be forced to make small talk with hundreds of people in only a matter of hours, not to mention playing nice with a particular client he was hoping to sign...

He was dreading it like most people did the dentist.

"Oh, don't be such a snob," his partner Desmond Haddad had said dismissively, when Laurence had complained earlier.

Desmond was everything Laurence was not—youthful, flashy, and bafflingly optimistic. He was tall, slim, and debonair, in contrast to Laurence's solid, grave steadiness, and always up for a party, when all Laurence really cared to do was work. Upon their arrival at JFK, Desmond had seized his friend's laptop, tablet, and work phone, despite Laurence's protests, then waved him off.

"It's for four hours," Desmond had said, mockingly. "You won't go drinking with me, I know that, so you might as well get some rest, look fresh for tonight. Surely you can make do without looking at a single ad campaign for four hours? Come on, Laurence. I find it hard to believe you grew up rich. You work as if you're millions of dollars in debt."

*Yes, fine.* He'd grown up fairly well off. After all, he'd met Desmond at Exeter. Hardly a high school for the impoverished, although his senator father's fortune paled in comparison to Desmond's dynastic oil money. Still, he could not explain to Desmond, who spent the money from his family coffers with gleeful abandon, the need to make a fortune that was completely his. And even when he *did* try to explain—

"Yeah, yeah, yeah…poor little rich boy, innit?" Desmond always said scornfully, his English accent cutting like glass. "Your problem, Laurence, is that you're too damned serious."

Well. Perhaps he was.

Laurence was relieved to see that the dining room was empty, except for a young woman seated alone at a table in front of a large stone fireplace.

"Do you mind, sir?" A harried-looking waiter ushered him to a table close to the young woman's. "We're short on staff right now, as there's an event taking place in a couple of hours. They've closed off most of the dining room."

"Very well."

It mattered little to him, and as the waiter fussed about with clean linen and water glasses, and a long, rambling recitation of the wine list, he found his eyes lingering idly on his dining room companion. She was tucking into an enormous meal with so much enjoyment he stifled a smile. She hadn't skimped on quality, either. On her table he identified the remains of a caviar starter, oysters, and a steak smothered in fresh mustard greens.

"Sir?"

He blinked, looked up. "A glass of whisky and water, please. And those oysters—" He gestured at the young lady's table. "Are they grilled?"

"Rockefeller style, sir."

"I'll have those, and the new potatoes in cream."

"Very good, sir."

The waiter swanned off, and Laurence was left to feel annoyed at the fact that he'd have to log into his email manually, since his rarely used personal phone had none of the many apps he used to keep his work organized. He hadn't used it in a couple of weeks, and he felt a rush of physical relief as he switched it on and began to scroll.

He was halfway through a report on viewing statistics for a motorbike ad when the waiter came back with a bread basket, dropped it off with little ceremony, and headed over to the young woman's table.

"Are we all set, then, ma'am?" he heard the waiter say solicitously.

Laurence listened with half an ear; he was curious to hear what such a voracious eater's voice sounded like.

"I am, thank you."

She spoke quietly, almost inaudibly. Her voice possessed a low husk that, despite himself, made him look up. It was familiar, in that elusive kind of way that nagged until finally the brain identified it. He registered wide eyes in the clearest shade of brown he'd ever seen, a full, bow-shaped mouth painted berry-red, and a dimpled chin before he looked back down at his phone.

*Pretty*, he thought idly. He'd look up again when she stood, see if the body matched the face. And there it was again—that sense of déjà-vu. Who could she possibly be? He'd gone to university abroad, so that was out. She looked far too young—and too broke—to be a client. Perhaps one of the many interns who filtered in and out of Laurence & Haddad each summer? No, it couldn't be that; he avoided them like the plague.

"Shall I charge it to your room, ma'am?"

"Oh, yes, please." Again, in that soft, cultured voice. "I'm in Suite 700."

"Ah, the penthouse. Very good, ma'am."

At *that*, Laurence did look up. He knew for sure that the woman wasn't staying in Suite 700, because that was *his* room.

Brazenly, she signed the bill with a flourish, and took a long, last sip of champagne with every indication of pleasure before looking up. She had the gall to shoot him a shy smile and lowered her lashes, touching the napkin to those soft, full lips.

Laurence was torn between being amused, annoyed, and appalled. If the menu was any indication, she'd just charged at least a few hundred to his room, and the little grifter hadn't even blinked.

He half considered going after her, but his phone buzzed just at that moment. His last impression was of subtle but definite curves shrouded in soft faded denim as she headed toward the door, hips swaying gently.

Laurence cleared his throat and looked away. He glanced down at the message, and what he saw was enough to drive all thoughts of beautiful, dinner-scamming women from his head.

"What the *hell* do you mean, you're in Dubai?" Laurence demanded. The dining room was thankfully still empty, so he didn't bother to leave. "Aurelia?"

On the other end of the line Aurelia Hunter—*his girlfriend*—yawned, and loudly. Laurence did a mental calculation: Dubai was nine hours ahead of New York. Most importantly, it was much too far away for her to show up that evening in formal dress as expected.

"Aurelia!"

"Hold on."

Aurelia sounded irritated now. He heard rustling—bedclothes, probably—and her soft dulcet tones speaking to someone else. Then she came back, sounding only slightly more awake.

*"What?"*

"You're. Supposed. To. Be. Here," Laurence said, emphasizing each word. "What do you mean, *what*?"

There was an incredulous pause, then Aurelia began to laugh. Loudly. "Are you serious?"

He was serious. He was also convinced that he was missing something very, very important.

"This is hardly a laughing matter," he snapped. "We're seated with the Muellers during coffee, Aurelia, and you know how important that account is—"

Her laughter finished on a gasp. "You really have no idea, do you?"

"Not unless you choose, very *kindly*, to fill me in. Why are you in Dubai?"

Aurelia's voice changed from incredulous amusement to something he was more familiar with: a studied coolness. "I see you didn't get any of my messages. I *know* you didn't return my calls."

"Obviously not," Laurence snapped.

He fumbled with the phone and opened his text notifications. Immediately messages began flashing up on the screen—messages that he hadn't checked. He squinted down at the screen, mouthing the words as he read them, then swore eloquently.

"Charming. I see you've seen it."

Laurence hated being taken by surprise, but this was outrageous in the extreme. "You're— *ending* this?"

She sighed. "I'm sorry, Laurence."

"Via *text message*?"

She snorted. "How else was I supposed to do it? You've been fielding my calls all week. Not much of a boyfriend, are you?" she added sarcastically. "And, as good as your assistant is at making you look genuinely busy, she isn't *that* good. I'm not going to fall for the 'in a meeting' line more than three times."

"But why?"

"I met someone."

Laurence stared at the screen, struck dumb. His arrangement with old school friend Aurelia Hunter had lasted a year and was quite a satisfactory one. As the head of a massive tech company she'd inherited from her father, she had no time to date but plenty of occasions for which a date was needed. A chance meetup at a networking party had led to their deal. He'd beau her around to her events, and she'd come to his, smile for photographs, be an escort he didn't have to worry about or call.

That last detail had apparently been his downfall.

Aurelia spoke into the silence. "I'm sorry. I— It's kind of been happening for a month, and it came to a head a week ago. I— It's different. I don't want to do this anymore. I sent you an email so you could make arrangements for the rest of the season."

Laurence scrolled through the email, biting back another litany of curses. Were he calmer, he might marvel at Aurelia's tone. She sounded softer than he'd ever heard her, both in the email and now, on the phone.

*She's really in love.*

He'd be happy for her, he supposed, if she hadn't screwed him over so colossally.

"That's all well and good," he said sarcastically, "and I hope you're enjoying your desert getaway, but this is *appalling*, Aurelia. I'm courting a huge client tonight, I've got events coming up, and—"

"Go solo."

She was definitely awake now—and possibly enjoying this? He heard the flick of a lighter, and Aurelia drew a long breath. He pictured her as she exhaled, probably swathed in something outrageously expensive, playing with the tendrils of hair on her shoulders.

"And if you do find someone else to do this with answer her calls, emails and texts, okay?"

"You really don't understand how badly you've messed things up for me, do you?"

Or maybe she had, until love had snatched all reason from her. Clients liked doing business with folks who were settled, committed. Couples were comforting. It made them feel as if their accounts were safe in the hands of someone who understood relationships, understood what it meant to make someone happy, to care for someone.

Laurence did not understand relationships or want to—he'd given that up long ago. But he knew what they looked like, and he knew what he needed to do to play that role. The idea of pursuing a woman for romantic reasons was out. He had no time or inclination for that. Aurelia had been an ideal compromise: no strings, no sex, none of the messy aftermath. Still, now the faithless woman had—

"Look, Laurence—"

Laurence hung up, then scrolled to her name and blocked her. It was childish, he knew, but he had a problem to solve and Aurelia was no longer relevant. He could explain away her absence tonight, but the rest of the season still lay before him, with all the galas, the dinner parties, the weekends away—

He swore under his breath again. She'd *met* someone. Women! They really were the most *ridiculous* creatures.

If Kitty Asare knew one thing, it was that lies were much more convincing when she half believed them herself. So she recited them over and over again as she stood shivering in the ladies' lounge at the Park Hotel. It was cold—colder than she'd anticipated—but then again, all she was wearing was a black lace thong at the moment.

She unzipped the small rolling backpack she'd brought with her and extracted the silk dress inside, then held it up critically to the light. Last season's, of course, obtained from one of those designer dress rental sites. It didn't look too terribly off-season, she told herself. It suited her lanky frame and deep coloring, and had enough oomph for tonight's soiree without looking out of place. It was also in her favorite color: a deep Lincoln green with a hint of brightness that made the rich tints of her skin glow.

Blending in was essential, since she hadn't actually been invited. All that mattered was that she'd manage, for the fourth time that month, to run into Sonia Van Horn at a New York social event.

She was counting on Sonia being in a good mood. The kindly middle-aged woman was definitely a low-watt bulb, but she was current chair of the board of the Hunt Society—a social club that Kitty had been trying to get into for a year and a half.

The small, unobtrusive group of the *ton* on the outskirts of Long Island was made up of a number of appallingly horsy middle-aged people, but it was one of the oldest, finest clubs in the state, and Kitty was determined to begin moving intimately with that group—or at the very least get an audience with them. There were simply too many potential contacts there to ignore—contacts with fat wallets who liked the convenience of contributing to a cause without getting their jeweled hands dirty.

Quality over quantity, she told herself as she shimmied the dress over her slender hips. As founder of a foundation that helped foster children transition to real life, Kitty had learned over the years that cold-calling and mass-mailing brochures was not enough. The charities she'd studied that achieved the most were either established by wealthy patrons or fronted by them, with endowments in the billions. A one-time donation was not nearly as beneficial as a lifetime supporter—and Kitty wanted those lifetime supporters.

She yanked the zipper up, trying to get her shivering under control. The dress fit okay, but narrow straps held up a draped bodice that was just a hair too big. Kitty would have to remember to stay upright.

*Rich people*, she thought with some disgust, and as she did so she saw the strong line of her jaw jut out from beneath the skin in soft relief. She'd have to take deep breaths, settle her face before she went in.

She knew from experience that the grasping, greedy bunch inside would have spent months— and millions—planning their jewelry, their impeccably tailored wardrobes. Makeup and hair would have been done by professionals hours before, and they would have been ferried to the Park Hotel from their Manhattan penthouses and their Long Island and Connecticut mansions to a party where champagne would flow like bath water.

Kitty, of course, had no such resources. She'd done her hair herself, cringing at the heat while she hot-combed her hair as close to her scalp as she could, and her dress would need to be dropped into a mailbox before noon on Monday if she wanted to avoid a fee from the rental company. There was no such thing as a fairy godmother—not for Kitty Asare. She had to make her own transformation.

*Not that I care*, she reminded herself.

She didn't want to be one of them. Years ago she'd reached for the moon and fallen hard, and Kitty, if nothing else, was someone who learned from her mistakes. Hope was futile; so was depending on people. She didn't need any of them. She just needed their money, and she needed plenty of it.

Kitty had an encyclopedic memory for names, faces and stories, and she used them shamelessly. Acquaintances became donors much faster than strangers did, and though the glitter of these people was nothing but a pretty facade on an aching emptiness, their money was extremely useful.

Other than that, the thought of all the opulence, the waste, left a bad taste in Kitty's mouth. There were people only a few zip codes away who had nothing tonight—not even a bed to sleep in. There had been a time when she'd been one of those people, and she'd been angry at the injustice of it, but now she chose to use what she'd learned over the years to take some of that money and funnel it to where it was really needed: to support the underserved.

People like the girl she'd been.

Kitty took a deep and steadying breath. She could not think of that—not right now. Thinking of what she'd lost and how she'd lost it made her stomach clench and her eyes water, even ten years later. She would not be able to maintain her composure if she dwelled on it too much.

*Focus*, she told herself.

She looked the part, she'd dressed the part, and she'd fortified herself with a meal fit for a king. She smiled, thinking of the meal she'd charged to the penthouse suite. It was immature, but it felt like sticking it to the Man, just a little, in a gloriously Robin Hoodish manner.

There had been another diner in the room, ordering a meal as lavish as hers had been. *He probably didn't even finish it*, Kitty thought, with a mixture of wistfulness and disdain. He'd been shrouded in shadows from the soft lighting in the room, but she'd been able to make out broad shoulders, smooth skin, fine tailored clothes. Someone accustomed to that sort of life. Probably handsome, too—they always were.

A glance at the time reminded her that she needed to head over to the Grand Ballroom—and now. Experience had taught her it was much easier to sneak into an event of this magnitude a bit late, when people were liquored up, security guards were relaxed, and groups were moving in and out.

She looked in the mirror. She should take pleasure in her appearance. The dress skimmed over her slim figure and her makeup was done to perfection. However, her eyes looked wide and anxious—too anxious. There was an odd prickling beneath her skin, as if something were about to happen.

*For heaven's sake, they're just people.*

Kitty picked up her beaded clutch. She'd stow her overnight bag with the concierge until the event was over and she was stumbling out to the subway to head back to Queens. She straightened her thin shoulders, set her face, and clattered out the door, moving seamlessly into a group of well-dressed, heavily perfumed people heading for the ballroom.

The soiree, Kitty knew, was "a little dinner and dance" for clients of an advertising firm that Sonia's husband worked for. Enormous floor-to-ceiling prints and digital screens showcased what she supposed were the focuses of the firm: whiskies, wines, a couple of luxury cars, perfumes, watches. Most of the women in the room wore gowns and cocktail dresses in deep greens and maroons and golds, echoing the runways of that year—she'd at least got that right.

Her mouth went dry as she identified several people she knew—well, not personally, but she knew of them. Page Six, the society columns, TMZ even. She needed to find Sonia, and she needed to do it now.

She pulled out her phone and shot the older woman a quick text message.

Hi, heard from a little birdie that you're at the Laurence & Haddad event tonight! Are you anywhere about? Would love to say hello. :)

She hit "send," knowing it was probably futile. She was fairly positive the fifty-two-year-old matron wouldn't have it out at an event like this one.

Suddenly she felt tired, and prickles of what felt suspiciously like embarrassment heated her neck, bit under her arms. It was the dreadful, suffocating self-consciousness of a person who didn't belong, and it would choke her if she let it. Audacity was probably the defining characteristic of people who were successful at this, and normally she had plenty. Tonight she didn't know what was wrong with her. Perhaps it was the heavy meal she'd had earlier.

She tossed her head and held it high, determined to overcome it.

And then she saw *him*.

The man from the dining room.

She'd only seen him for a few minutes before clearing out of the room to dress, but she certainly had noticed him—it had been hard not to. Now that he was standing, and she could see him from head to toe, she felt that same, almost involuntary prickle of excitement, beginning at her scalp and blossoming down.

He was big and solidly muscled, and the simple black tuxedo he wore created sleek lines from broad shoulders to a narrow waist. He was drinking champagne and surveying the room with a critical eye. He looked as if he did not quite approve of something.

She would not call him handsome—his features were too irregular for that. However, he was undeniably attractive…something that was unsettling for Kitty. She remembered the dark, heady gaze he'd directed at her from his table and she swallowed, then gathered her wits and began to walk toward him.

When she was close enough, she stopped and used the full battery of her eyes on him. "Hello," she said, simply.

When the man turned and looked at her Kitty experienced such a surge of unexpected warmth that she felt quite weak. The warmth was chased by panic when she looked at his face. She was now able to make out features far sharper than the hazy impression a candlelit dining room had left. Close up...

*She knew him.*

His was a face that was connected to her past, to the things that still kept her up at night even after ten years.

Kitty felt her whole body go hot, all the way to her fingertips. She tried in one frantic effort to make her face stony, but she knew he had seen that moment of panic. She opened her mouth, his name on her lips, but he beat her to it.

*This could not possibly get any worse.*

"I'm Laurence Stone," he said, "and I think it's time for you to leave."

# CHAPTER TWO

"LAURENCE *STONE?*" KITTY WHISPERED.

His lips curved up. "So you've heard of me."

Heard of him? She *knew* him. She'd met him only once before, at a party not unlike this one, in the massive mansion in Long Island where she'd been living with his parents. Laurence Stone. Only son of one of the sitting senators in the state of New York, or he had been in those days.

Kitty had been there as a foster child, connected to the Stones through his wife's involvement with the state's social services department. She'd been living with them for the year when Laurence had arrived on Christmas break from his place at boarding school, and they'd met at the annual New Year's party there.

Before she'd been thrown out of the house. For reasons she could not dwell on now, or she would not get out of this room without looking insane.

*Laurence Stone.*

As her mind raced, she was able to process how much he'd changed. She remembered him as a teenager—a big angled handsome one, handsome enough to make her seventeen-year-old heart flutter, but still a teenager. The man in front of her had grown both up and out, and what had been a rather devilish jauntiness had matured into something else entirely. He was tall—tall and broad enough to make her feel rather slight. Not an easy feat for a girl who nearly stood six feet tall in her stockinged feet.

He didn't say anything. He just looked down at her with a distinct lack of expression.

Prickles of embarrassment began to flood her neck and cheeks with warmth.

"Well?" he said finally, and the baritone rumbling from his chest seemed to penetrate every sensory nerve she had.

She took a full step back, and at that his mouth jerked upward…just a slight twitch.

He'd noticed.

She swallowed. His eyes slid down the length of her, from the crown of her head to the twenty-dollar stilettos on her feet. She felt all at once that he'd stripped her naked—not to violate her, but to assess the net worth of her outfit, if not her life, in ten seconds flat.

*He doesn't recognize me.*

Kitty had never been more grateful to have been little and scrawny in high school, with close-cropped dark hair that in no way resembled the jet-black waves that spilled past her shoulders now.

"I saw you in the dining room earlier, and…" She faltered.

*Get out of here!*

He smiled. It wasn't a nice smile. "And?"

"And I thought I'd come over and say hello." Kitty forced her shoulders back and lifted her chin. Who did he think he was, looking at her as if she'd crawled out from under a not too impressive rock? "Clearly," she said, a little haughtily, "you're busy. So I can make my way—"

"I saw you, too," he said, and with gleeful precision he moved in for the kill.

His voice dropped an octave, and despite her irritation Kitty's stomach did too, pooling somewhere low in her abdomen. She shifted uncomfortably, pressed her thighs together.

"Did you enjoy your dinner?" he asked.

"My…?"

"You know," he said, "when I confronted the front desk about my suddenly astronomical dining bill I was almost pleasantly surprised. You've got exquisite taste for a thief. Osetra caviar, champagne and peppered Kobe steak?"

Kitty swore. It was involuntary, but the word slipped out before she could stop it, and Laurence's left brow climbed to join its twin. She closed her eyes—this could *not* be happening.

"Charming," he drawled. "I think it was rather rude not to ask me to join you, considering you knew my room number." His face raked over her face and form again, but it was questioning this time rather than mocking. "And you look so damned familiar. I just can't place—"

"Laurence?"

An older man's voice interrupted them and they both turned. The mixture of amusement and irritation completely left her companion's face and it changed as suddenly as a thundercloud might give way to the sun during a tropical storm.

"Giles!" Laurence said heartily. He reached out and clapped the man on the back, then began to walk away with him.

She was forgotten. At least for the moment.

In one quick motion she whirled and, despite the heels, ran back the way she had come. Forget Sonia. She needed to get her bag and get on the subway as fast as her feet could carry her.

\* \* \*

Laurence quickly forgot the young woman and her frightened face. As usual, business drove thoughts of anything else from his mind.

"I'm gonna be straight with you," Giles Mueller said, with that annoyingly gruff cheer he wielded like an instrument of torture.

"Go right ahead!" Now even *he* sounded idiotic. He sighed inwardly. Desmond was nowhere to be found.

"First of all, how's the Senator? Wonderful things he's doing out there!"

"He's peachy," Laurence said, no longer able to hold back his sarcasm.

"Wonderful, wonderful… Laurence?" Giles said, and his face changed. "Perhaps a moment or two?"

Laurence nodded in assent. "At least let me get you a drink, Giles."

One snap of the fingers and a server appeared with two servings of Japanese whisky, courtesy of their latest client.

Giles made an appreciative noise deep in his throat as he sipped. "Exceptional."

Laurence watched him, a pleasant half-smile still in place. Over his years in the business Laurence had identified several different types of clients. Giles was the type who adored being wooed. Desmond was better at the wooing, and Laurence usually left it to him, but an account of the Muellers' standing was one that could not be left to chance.

The man owned a private racetrack that was a new but significant player in the horse-racing industry on the Eastern seaboard, and his goal was to blow the walls off the old clubs, making the sport as mainstream as baseball. Giles had the track, the connections, the money—what he needed was an advertising firm that would create an enormous buzz, fill the stands at his racetrack with the people he wanted.

Laurence's father, the Senator, loved horses as well. The old jackass was good for mostly nothing, but at least thanks to him Laurence knew enough about the sport to have caught Giles's attention weeks ago, when he and Desmond made their pitch. Now Giles was dancing them on a string, enjoying being courted before making the decision Laurence knew he'd made already. Tonight, the thought of Aurelia's defection had soured the chase considerably.

"Very much looking forward to seeing you at the track next weekend, Laurence." Giles sipped his drink with every indication of enjoyment on his florid face, pursing his lips in a silent whistle of appreciation.

"Not as much as me, Giles." Laurence cleared his throat. "I'm looking forward to seeing your track again. My father infinitely prefers it to Belmont."

The words were bitter in his mouth, but the thought of Giles's millions made them drift out as smoothly as watered silk. However he voted, an endorsement from a prominent politician would flatter—exactly as Laurence intended it would.

Giles's chest puffed out with pride. "He's too kind. Please, do give him our regards—and let him know there's a private box for him whenever he graces us with his presence again."

"Absolutely, Giles."

*When pigs fly. Or horses.*

There was no way, of course, for Giles to know he hadn't spoken to his father in years, but that was a conversation he wasn't interested in having.

"Very well then, Laurence, we'll see you soon. I'm looking forward to giving you a tour of the place…hearing your ideas. Doris has some amusement planned for the womenfolk, too, so tell your lady-friend."

"I will," Laurence said, more sourly than he would have liked, remembering Aurelia.

He could not tell Giles that said "lady-friend" was no more. Doris Mueller was nervous and exact—precisely the sort of hostess who'd go into a snit if her dinner table was suddenly uneven. Besides, that would open up a whole slew of questions he wasn't ready to answer. Thankfully the Muellers had never actually met Aurelia, so at least there was that.

He patted the man's shoulder, gesturing to a server to top up his glass. "We'll be there," he said, and he shot Giles Mueller the smile that had closed a thousand deals. He needed some fresh air. "We can't wait."

Laurence took his fresh air as soon as he could.

From the outside, the Park Hotel looked very different from its posh interior. It was undergoing restoration on the magnificent Gilded Age French doors on the balconies of the rooms facing the street, and rusting gray scaffolding hugged either side of the main entrance, but it was such a common sight in New York City that no one blinked.

The wind had picked up, and Laurence ducked under the plastic sheeting that was draped on the sides of the scaffolding that served as a divider for a temporary walkway. He stared out at the street, irritated at the fact that he felt irritated. He did not want, *need* to feel anything but indifference.

When a woman emerged from the doorway of the Park Hotel and joined him in his temporary shelter he started in surprise.

*Again?*

"You," he said.

He felt his annoyance at Aurelia melt away; this was a welcome distraction. And what an attractive distraction she was, he noted, taking his time to look her up and down again, indolently. In the dining room she'd been wearing a hideous sweatshirt and nondescript jeans; this dress, he'd noticed inside, definitely showed off more of her. Long legs topped by slender thighs were outlined by the clinging skirt. Her braless breasts were high, full, and very visible beneath thin fabric.

To his delight she started to squirm, and suddenly looked too warm. Her hands were trembling. He wasn't sure if it was from the cold or from the lie, but he didn't care. If she was bold enough to charge Kobe beef and a bottle of Perrier-Jouet to a total stranger's room, she should be bold enough to face the consequences.

He took a step closer to her. She did not step back, but her chest rose and fell a bit more rapidly. Laurence was close enough now to smell rosewater and something else, something richer, reminiscent of perfumed oil warmed by soft skin. It hung around her like a scented mantle, and if he did not step back right away it might be because he was trying to identify the complex scent.

He did like a good perfume, if it suited the wearer, and this one did. Gentle, insistent, without being cloying on skin that looked so soft he suddenly itched to touch it. He wondered…just a thought…what she might do if he pressed the backs of his fingers to the slender column of her throat, felt the pulse he saw beating wildly there. There was an odd feeling of intimacy that hung between them… He definitely had seen her before. But where?

The next few things happened so quickly he did not have time to process them. The young woman's face was suddenly contorted in shock. There was a faint rattling directly above his head, and then a full-bodied shove from her, so hard he stumbled backwards.

She'd knocked him off his feet completely!

The two of them tumbled into the busy street.

Behind them he heard a creak, a groan, and a crash, but right now all he was concentrating on was not getting run over by the worst of post-dinner Manhattan traffic. He blindly reached out, dragged her into his arms, rolled over. He heard a soft cry of pain, but that couldn't be helped at the moment. All he thought of was shielding her.

Feet away from them he heard screams and shouts and raised his head. The scaffolding they'd been standing under collapsed to the ground in a spectacular avalanche of dust and steel.

# CHAPTER THREE

*LAURENCE STONE.*

"I don't know why you won't let me take you to the hospital," he growled.

The name throbbed through her head to the rhythm of the headache that was forming. They had almost died and she'd *saved him*.

"I told you, my insurance doesn't cover ER visits."

Kitty swallowed hard and closed her eyes. The first thing she'd croaked when he'd dragged her to the curb, ignoring the myriad drivers cursing them out, was, "No ambulance," and Laurence Stone had been *furious*.

"That is no excuse," he snapped. "I'd pay, anyway. It's the least I could do, considering you kept me from being crushed."

"I won't let you pay—"

"You won't let me pay for a doctor, but you'll let me pay for your damned food? Now, don't move."

She felt large hands, surprisingly gentle, run over her back, her arms, her temples. She felt violently ill. It was as if she'd suddenly realized how close they'd come to death.

"Your teeth are chattering," he said, a bit less crisply.

In a moment he'd shrugged off his jacket and she was draped in the softest, finest quality material she'd ever felt in her life. It even smelled expensive, and that made her feel even dizzier. His face was still forbidding, but he drew the sides together with enough gentleness to make her eyes well up despite herself.

She closed them, not wanting the tears to come. Crying was not a luxury she afforded herself much. Kitty wanted nothing more than to lean on him, ease the pounding in her head, but he'd probably recoil and toss her right back in the road.

She was startled when she felt the warmth of his fingers. They skimmed over her left cheekbone as if to assess any damage done.

"Open your eyes," he ordered.

His voice was decisive, but at least that nasty lilt had left it, and he sounded almost kind.

When her eyes fluttered open, she swallowed.

"Are you hurt?" she managed from between numb lips.

Gosh, it seemed like the temperature had plunged ten degrees in the time it had taken for this to happen. It was early summer, early enough for the nights to still have some bite to them, but this was on another level.

"No, I'm not."

He hadn't a single scratch she could see. His tuxedo had escaped with only a little dirt streaking the knees.

"Anyway. Get up," he ordered, drawing back and shattering the moment.

She stared up at him.

"Come on."

He stood and extended a large hand. Even with all his bluster, she could see him shooting tense glances at the pile of rubble that would have buried him. People were beginning to emerge from the doorway, to stare at it, gasp, exclaim, pull out their cell phones.

"Let's get you upstairs and cleaned up."

"I'm sorry?" Kitty asked rather stupidly; it was hard to form words.

"Suite 700. I'm fairly certain you know it—you did bill a dinner to the room, after all."

Would he *stop* alluding to that? Kitty's indignation was just the shot of adrenaline she needed, and from the flicker of amusement on his face she suspected he knew it. She lifted her chin and attempted to stand, but her legs folded beneath her as if she was a newborn lamb.

She decided to stay put for the moment. "I am not coming upstairs with you, or anywhere else!"

"Don't be ridiculous." He frowned. "You just saved my life. I'm not going to repay you by taking advantage of you. And if you won't go to hospital, the least you can do is let me watch you. What if you've got a concussion?"

"I don't."

She hadn't hit her head, although blood was trickling down her arm. Her hip was sore, too, and most of the skin had come off her palms from where she'd used them to break her fall.

She probably had him to thank for her lack of really serious injuries. The moment they'd fallen he'd wrapped his arms around her and rolled. He'd *protected* her. She swallowed hard against a scratchy throat, wondering if she'd inhaled some of the gravel when she fell.

"Then come with me before the cameras get here." His eyes scanned the street and he groaned. "Hell. They're already here."

When she attempted to rise again, Laurence hissed through his teeth.

"Will you let me help you up, at least?"

She hesitated for a moment, then she nodded.

Laurence bent to anchor one large arm round her waist, pulling her to her feet. Even from this undignified position, she tried to muster all the haughtiness she could. "I don't need—"

"Like hell you don't," he said rudely, and began to walk, matching his long legs to Kitty's stride. Now that she'd emerged from the fog of shock, she took note of more elemental things: the feel of her cheek pressed to the softest dress shirt she'd ever felt, and the iron-hard muscle it covered.

"Are you all right?" he said after a moment.

She could hear his baritone rumbling low in his chest, and the sound of it stirred deep in her lower belly.

"It isn't far to the elevator."

"I'm fine."

"See that you don't trip, so I don't have to haul you up again. You women wear the most ridiculous shoes."

*A thank-you would be nice*, Kitty thought, dumbly letting him cart her through the double doors like a sack of flour.

She wondered if her tumble into the street had knocked all remaining sense out of her head and concluded that it probably had. That was the only explanation for why she huddled beneath his solid warmth and followed him so meekly. Perhaps she also did it because— Well. She did know him, after a fashion. He wasn't a complete stranger to her, even though there was no indication on his chiseled face that he'd ever met her in his life.

"Nothing to see here," he snapped at the throng that had collected. They scattered.

He bypassed the main elevators and rounded a corner, and then they were left alone in front of a private wood-paneled elevator. Laurence released her, saw that she was steady, and extracted a key fob from an inner pocket, which he pressed to the sensor.

In the few moments before the doors whooshed open Kitty had the opportunity to study him carefully, in a way she hadn't been able to in the poor light outside. His frame seemed to take up all the space. He had a narrow face topped by a head of tightly cropped ink-black hair. His lashes and brows were equally dark, and Kitty was suddenly struck by a memory: his eyes, soft and honey-brown, boring into hers as they spoke in soft candlelight in the ballroom of his parents' Long Island estate.

He'd been kind to her that night, taken her under his wing when she'd been overlooked, ignored by the glitterati flitting about and skimming the marble floor with feet as light as angels' wings. Kitty, young and innocent, had been thoroughly seduced by the elegance, and in despair of ever living up to it.

Laurence had crossed the ballroom and stopped in front of her, two glasses of pilfered wine in his hands—an unlikely Prince Charming in a fashionable designer suit.

"This is boring as hell," he'd said, a little indelicately, but tears had sprung to Kitty's eyes at the relief of being noticed.

They'd sipped the sticky wine and made awkward conversation, and at midnight, when bells had chimed soft and sweet, and every person in the room had turned to embrace their companions, he'd bent and kissed her on the cheek.

"Happy New Year," he'd told her a little gruffly, and she'd blushed. "I'm out of here."

And he had been gone in an instant, presumably to one of the many Manhattan parties that she hadn't been invited to.

She'd gone to bed as soon as she could get

away, snuggled beneath her down bedspread, replaying the memory. It had been a small kindness, but one that she'd held on to in those long lonely days, and it was the last happy memory she had of the Stone household.

Even now it still hurt…the way she'd been dismissed. The Senator—her foster father up until that point—hadn't said a word to her about it. She'd gone to her prep school as usual, about two weeks after the party, and Laurence had gone back to Exeter. One day when she'd opened the door of the car that normally picked her up, with its enormous leather seats and government plates, her case worker, Anna, had been in the back. Kitty's stomach had immediately dropped to her feet. As a long-timer in the system, she had known that an unexpected visit from a case worker meant nothing but upheaval.

"There's been…some complications, Katherine," Anna had said, wringing her soft hands. "I'm afraid you have to come with me."

There had been a trip back to the Stone mansion to collect her things, already waiting outside on the porch. There had been a trip to a lawyer's office where she had been asked to sign an NDA. She'd listened, dumbly, as the man droned on about not talking to the press and where she should direct questions and told her that, yes, the Senator was still planning on paying for four years at the college of her choice.

At that, Kitty's head had snapped up. "I don't want it."

"Katherine—" her case worker had entreated.

"No. I don't want it."

Even at seventeen years old, Kitty had known that something terrible was afoot, and she'd wanted no part of what she realized was bribery.

"I will honor the non-disclosure agreement. If Senator Stone thinks I've done something so terrible that he can't even give me the respect of telling me personally—"

"Katherine!"

By that time Kitty had been sobbing so hard she could barely breathe, but she'd insisted, adamantly, that she would *not*, under any circumstances, accept the money. She'd only stopped shouting when the lawyer had hurriedly drafted a document waiving her rights to the money. She'd wiped the snot off her face, signed it, and walked out of her Cinderella story.

She'd graduated from public school, gotten a scholarship to City College, and now she ran her own foundation—one that raised money to help youngsters in her situation. She'd been angry,

yes, for a long time, but she'd managed to chan-
nel those emotions into getting money for kids
like her—kids who needed the help. She'd been
around wealth for only a short time, but enough
to see how much it did for people—and how
much it emboldened them to be monsters. Kitty
now lived the simplest possible life, funneling
money to those who needed it by way of donations, grants…anything she could get her hands
on.

Tonight, this chance encounter with Laurence
Stone—now a man—had brought it all back to
her mind with devastating clarity.

When the elevator doors slid open, he gestured. "This is us," he said.

Kitty took in a breath.

The entryway led into a massive front parlor,
with a sunken floor and a lofty ceiling lined
with skylights—a meeting of old and new de-
sign. In the daytime the place would be flooded
with sunlight, but now she could see stars glit-
tering as brightly and as vastly as they would
have if she'd been outside. The interior had
stone-colored walls and soft plush rugs in dull
rusts, chocolates and siennas, all spread over a
polished wood floor. The furniture she couldn't
recognize, but she knew the style—very Eng-

lish, probably vintage, and undoubtedly worth a fortune.

Laurence turned his head when he didn't hear her footsteps behind him. "Well?" he asked, as he walked over to a rotary phone on a sofa table not too far away and grabbed the receiver. "I'll need a first-aid kit up here now, please," she heard him say. The sardonic voice was gone, replaced with a quiet authority that just screamed boardrooms and boarding schools. "And a bucket of ice..."

As he spoke, Kitty took a step, thought better of it, and then slid her feet out of her heels before creeping forward. She stood hesitantly in front of the sofa he'd indicated and began to sit—then popped up again. Her dress was filthy, never mind the blood still trickling from her shoulder. Maybe she should find a bathroom instead, and mop it up...

She jumped a little when the receiver clattered in its cradle and Laurence looked up, frowning when he took in her half-executed squat over the sofa cushions.

"What are you doing? Sit down."

"I don't want to mess up your sofa—" she began lamely.

"It isn't my sofa, it's the hotel's. Sit," he said, in

a voice that bore no argument, and then headed off into one of the side rooms.

When he came back he carried an ornate bottle, took it straight to the wet bar that occupied the north corner of the room. When she looked confused, a hint of a smile crossed his face.

"It's whisky." He took down two glasses and spun them before they hit the bar. "Japanese. Our newest client, so I've a case in my room waiting to go back to the office with me. I thought we'd toast life, since I nearly lost mine tonight. Plus, I've had an appalling evening," he added, almost to himself.

Kitty opened her mouth; nothing came out. He was twisting the bottle open, beginning to pour. "I..." she managed, then swallowed and tried again. "I don't..."

"You don't drink? That's a lie—not with the bottle of champagne you charged to this room earlier."

There he went with a reference to her dinner again. Kitty scowled. "This is hardly just a *room*," she snapped. "And if you're in it, you can definitely afford a bottle of champagne."

Her show of spirit made him turn around and lift both eyebrows. Kitty raised her chin. She should be terrified. Hell, first of all he was Senator Stone's son, and she had no idea what the ramifications of their meeting would be. She also didn't know if she could get arrested for her idiotic move earlier that evening, but there was something in those inscrutable familiar eyes that dissolved her fear.

It was… Yes, that was it again. It was faint, but unmistakable. He was *amused*. That made her feel better, if nothing else.

Laurence poured a couple fingers of whisky in each glass, then pressed one into her hand. He raised his, gave her another of those not-quite-smiles. "To good health," he said, and raised the glass to his mouth. He only wet his lips before placing it down. "I've had enough tonight," he muttered under his breath.

Kitty took a tiny sip and immediately began to choke. The whisky, while smooth, was much stronger than the cocktails she preferred.

Laurence opened his mouth to comment, but a ring at the elevator entrance had him getting up instead. Thank goodness. She watched from her seat, taking prim sips from her glass—it did taste better as she got used to it. A white-jacketed attendant entered and opened a large first-aid kit on a side table, then shook crushed ice into a silver urn-shaped bucket.

He gave Kitty a cursory glance. "Sir, do you need assistance with—?"

"Nope," Laurence replied, rifling through the kit.

He was already tugging on a pair of blue latex gloves that seemed far too small for his hands. He selected gauze and alcohol swabs and a tube of cream with great efficiency.

"Would you like any food sent up, sir?"

"She's eaten plenty," he said, with just enough of a lilt in his voice for Kitty to choke on her whisky again, then glare in his direction.

He carried the case over to Kitty and peered at her injured shoulder with real interest.

"Lower that strap," he said, and his fingers danced across her collarbone.

Kitty jerked forward, startled both at the touch and at the way her body tightened in response.

"What?" She squeezed her glass in a death grip.

"Just lower it. Don't have the vapors…you don't need to remove it." His voice was quiet, unhurried, as if he did this all the time. "Perhaps you can light the fire for us before you go?" he said to the attendant, who was still hovering. "The lady is shivering."

The man nodded, clearly glad for something

to do. A flick of a switch on the wall had flames roaring and crackling in the big fireplace, and then he left.

Kitty was shivering, but it wasn't climate related. Having Laurence Stone so close was suffocating in an arousing way, and she was certain he knew it.

Laurence made a low sound in his throat as he examined her wounds. He slid a long warm finger beneath the edge of her dress, tugging it down further. Kitty felt her lungs constrict in her chest, just for a moment, at the warm jolt of his fingers on her bare flesh. She could feel her back arch of its own volition and her nipples tighten. She was positive that he'd notice. The thin silk and her lack of a bra was doing nothing to hide them.

She shifted uncomfortably.

"Don't move," he said.

His eyes flickered down and Kitty blushed. He'd noticed, all right, if the mocking curve of his mouth was any indication.

Kitty closed her eyes and inhaled deeply—which was a mistake. Losing her sight only heightened her other senses, and now she smelled something whisky-sharp, combined with the spiciness of soap and cologne on warm skin.

The urge to lean into him, to simply give in to that warmth, was utterly overwhelming.

"You've got several nasty scrapes and some gravel inside one," he said, so quietly she could barely hear him. "This is going to hurt."

"It's fine," she gasped, and gulped down the rest of her drink.

It did hurt, but she wasn't going to give him the satisfaction of seeing her wince. She would welcome the pain—anything to counter the dull ache that was beginning, inexplicably, between her thighs. Instinctively she pressed them together. It was as if the adrenaline rush from their near-death experience had gone straight to her nether regions; she'd be squirming in a moment if this didn't stop.

"Do it," she said, and the breathiness in her voice made her swallow.

Laurence Stone, despite his trademark iron-fast control, was very uncomfortable at that moment.

The entire night, he thought, as he gently swabbed blood and debris from the gold-tinged silken plane of her increasingly bare skin, was a disaster. Aurelia's stunt had thrown him off, Laurence had almost *died*, and now...

He resolved to ignore how she held her body

tense, or the way the soft mounds of her breasts were thrust upwards as if in offering. Every nerve-ending in his body was humming—had been since this girl had shoved him out of harm's way.

*You almost died.*

Even with his eyes open he could still see the pile of rubble, sending clouds of dust, shards of glass and steel into the air. He could have been crushed. Or perhaps a stake or broken glass might have driven straight into his heart. Or perhaps he might have been left paralyzed, a shell of himself—

*Stop thinking.*

This confrontation with his own mortality had shaken him like nothing else had ever been able to lately. Laurence was a planner. His life was a series of carefully calculated assessments of risk, benefit, and payoff. This had been a freak accident, and nothing rattled Laurence more than things he could not anticipate or control.

To keep from dwelling on this he had to concentrate on something else—and for now, unfortunately for her that was the supple curves of the dark-haired beauty pressing her knees together on the sofa next to him.

The young woman was clearly distressed—so

much so that Laurence felt quite sorry for her. However, once she'd settled into the plush uphol-stery and lowered the straps of the green dress she wore, all the tension of the evening had gone straight to his groin.

Her soft, rapid breathing did not help. Neither did the proximity of his fingers to the soft swell of bare skin. She was slim, yes—much slimmer than he usually preferred—but everything about her promised *lushness*. One tug, he thought, and the soft bounty of her breasts would be com-pletely exposed to him, to touch, to taste—

"Stop." He found himself saying it out loud, more to himself than to her, really, but her eyes fluttered open again anyway, and he was con-fronted by that lovely shade of brown.

He could see it in her eyes, reflected as clearly as his own face.

*Mutual desire.*

And she wasn't schooled enough to hide it—another key difference from the woman who'd just dumped him.

Laurence cleared his throat and pulled back, making quick work of fastening a clean white gauze bandage round her upper arm. She began to speak very carefully, as if she were trying not to slur her words. Another reason for him to get her out of here as quickly as possible.

"Y'know, it's rude to make a lady drink alone…"

Laurence laughed out loud, hoping the sound would drive out some of the tension and it did—somewhat. He picked up his glass and downed the liquid as coolly as he might a glass of water.

She goggled. "How is your throat not on fire?"

"I've likely had more practice than you." Laurence slid a finger underneath her shoulder strap and tugged it back into place, careful not to put pressure on the wounded area. She quivered, ever so slightly, and he tempered his gruffness. For now.

"The bandage doesn't really go with the dress, but you can consider yourself patched up." He decanted another measure of whisky into a glass. He offered it to his companion first, but she shook her head.

"I think I'd better have water this round," she said a little primly, and he laughed.

He took a long sip, closing his eyes, feeling the smooth slide down his throat. The whisky was so smooth it would not burn…not until it had settled deep in his stomach. He leaned his head against the back of the sofa. He really should get up, but something in him wanted to savor this moment, this quiet.

They sat in silence; then she spoke, softly. "We almost died."

"We did," he attested, "but we didn't. And you mustn't think that way. If you do, you'll never want to walk under scaffolding again."

She frowned. "You cannot be okay with this."

"I'm alive; what more do I want?"

She turned her head.

"Hey," he said gently.

The young woman was biting her lower lip hard. He leaned forward and pressed his thumb to the dimple in her chin, dislodging the soft wet skin from her teeth. It had plumped from her abuse and was redder than her lipstick could make it.

"You're alive," he said firmly, and there was some compassion in his voice. They did have that bond of survival, after all. "We're alive. Celebrate it and move on."

She opened her mouth and closed it—and then there was nothing else. Because suddenly the softness of her body was pressed full against his and she was kissing him.

# CHAPTER FOUR

*DECADENT.*

That was the first word that came to mind when Kitty pressed her lips to Laurence's. He was surprised. She felt him stiffen and grow rigid. The inside of Kitty's head was awash with panic, even as her lips softened, parted.

*What the hell are you doing?*

She was, she realized, trying to grasp something, anything, that would assuage this tension that was winding her body taut. She'd drunk just enough whisky and it'd gone to her head just fast enough to ensure that she would do something this stupid. And now that she was kissing him—

He was kissing her back.

It was controlled, and very, very short, but it was enough for her to taste alcohol and spice and send a jolt of lust through the haze that threatened to lift her straight off the sofa.

"Please…" she whispered against his lips.

The sound of her voice broke whatever spell

they both were under. A moment later he began pulling back, leaving Kitty trying to steady her breath. His eyes were carefully blank, but there was enough storminess in his expression to keep Kitty's pulse racing.

*He wants you.*

That in itself was something she'd never thought a possibility: the thought that Laurence Stone might ever want *her*.

"Are you all right?" he said after a moment, in a carefully neutral tone. "You've had a lot to drink."

Heat rushed to Kitty's face instantly. She knew exactly what that meant. Pulling herself together, she somehow managed to stand. She was relieved that the room did not spin, neither did she wobble. She licked her lips; she could still taste him on them.

"I'm sorry," she said after a moment.

"For what?" Laurence's face was as calm as if she were apologizing for bumping into him in a supermarket. "We went through a traumatic event tonight. Let's not speak of it anymore."

Kitty should be grateful he seemed so determined to forget, but instead she felt a rush of anger that shocked her in its intensity. She was being dismissed. She was always being dismissed.

*Now you're being irrational. He doesn't even know who you are.*

Kitty swallowed hard once, twice, three times, and dignity reached out its strong arm to steady her.

*You need to get out of here.*

The past had come back for her in the form of the son of the man who'd cast her out so unceremoniously. And she, overcome by the present and the fact that she'd nearly lost her life, had lost all self-control and kissed him.

When she thought back on it, tears threatened to well up in her eyes—tears of humiliation at her own behavior. Ordering the meal... How could she have given in to such a stupid, *childish* impulse? Despite her show of strength, Kitty was not made of stone, and in quiet moments over the past ten years she'd often daydreamed of running into the Stones as a polished, successful woman...an *equal*.

Tonight had been the opposite of that.

Silence hung heavy over them for a few moments; then Laurence spoke quietly. "Let's go. I'll put you in a car."

Kitty blinked hard, nodded, shoved her feet

into her shoes. The two of them made their way to the elevator, entered at the touch of a button and faced each other, silent.

Laurence broke the silence first. "You'll have to let me do something to pay you back," he said.

She shook her head. Someone with Laurence's millions—billions, probably—would be an ideal sponsor, but she wanted nothing more than to exit his life and forget she'd met him. Again.

Gooseflesh rose up on her arms; instinctively she rubbed at them. Laurence saw this, and in a moment she was once again draped in the heavy softness of his jacket.

"No—" she tried to protest.

"Just wear it. You can give it back to me downstairs." He crossed his arms.

When the doors whooshed open, light assaulted her retinas and she blinked. Her time upstairs with Laurence seemed like an encounter from a different land…a candlelit land with whisky and soft kisses and the strong clean scent of him that now clung to her skin, blending perfectly with her own.

A couple stood in front of the public elevators—an older couple, dressed in dour but very correct evening dress. She recognized the man after a moment. He was the same one who had been talking to Laurence in the Grand Ballroom. When he saw them the man's eyes lit up, and Kitty thought she heard Laurence swear...very quietly.

"Laurence! Is this your lady-friend?" the man said effusively.

Kitty gasped, for Laurence's arm had snaked out to draw her close to his side. He spoke quickly, with increasing pressure on her hand that set out a clear message: *Be silent.*

"It certainly is," Laurence said smoothly, and his dark eyes glittered with a sudden intensity that shut Kitty up much faster than his silent imploring had.

His next words froze her in place, sent a shock through her.

"Giles, this is Katherine Asare. She appeared rather unexpectedly tonight, and she's been *dying* to meet you."

# CHAPTER FIVE

"YOUR *LADY-FRIEND*?" Katherine demanded, prodding his arm. Hard.

The trembling waif who'd kissed him only minutes ago had been replaced with an indignant woman, demanding answers. Laurence ignored her.

The two of them were outside now, waiting for his car to pull round. The rubble that had nearly buried them was now roped off with sheets of plastic and orange strips that warned *Caution*.

He shook his head. He had plenty to be cautious about, and Katherine Asare had made it to the top of the list in a single leap. The fact that he'd impulsively dragged her into the Giles matter was another layer of complication he didn't need. He rarely acted so rashly. He did not like this at all. And the girl, with her incessant questioning, was not letting him think.

She wouldn't be the first woman from his past to reappear as if by chance, and the fact that she'd kissed him— Suspicion was fast overwhelming his initial curiosity.

"Why would you tell him that?" she said, punctuating her words with a stamp of her foot. "Can you hear me?"

Of course he could hear her—she was shrieking in his ear, after all. He turned slightly.

"And don't lift your eyebrows!"

They, of course, climbed.

"Why didn't you tell me who you were?" he countered. "You knew it was me as far back as the ballroom."

The shot was an accurate one; her eyes dropped in confusion. "I—"

*Little Katherine Asare.*

He'd known there was something familiar about her the minute he'd seen her in the ballroom that evening—but he hadn't remembered who she was until she'd kissed him, pulled back, and looked up at him with those massive dark eyes. Then recognition had slammed him in the gut; he'd barely been able to hide it.

The more she spoke, the clearer a picture of the timid teenager he remembered stood out in his head. He vaguely remembered skinny arms and legs, a deplorably flat chest, a jaw far too strong for her face, black hair cropped close to her head, and again those vivid eyes—her most distinctive feature, but so shadowed by anxiety that she'd always looked haunted.

He raked his memory for information. She'd been his parents' little foster foundling from Ghana. She'd been brought on board as the first recipient of his father's foray into philanthropy, all to appeal to a certain group of voters and to give his ex-supermodel wife something more meaningful to do than be photographed spending thousands at the French boutiques she favored. Some tragic backstory, if he remembered rightly—dead parents and a granny who'd been deported when she was small.

They'd brought her into the household months before his father's election campaign had launched, doubtless to ensure that his father was painted in the most sympathetic, most benevolent, most philanthropic light, and his mother had gone along with his hypocrisy like she always did.

*Could the man have been any more transparent?*

His lip curled in disgust at the memory. A common schoolgirl, an orphan, no family in the United States. A girl with ties to his own mother's native Ghana—a tacit reminder that his father had married just as open-mindedly as he'd chosen a foster child. A perfect complement to his mixed-race son, whom he trotted out for events like a dumb, obedient show puppy, but ignored otherwise!

Laurence had come home for Christmas break that year, angry and resentful, and his discovery of the real reason Katherine had been brought into their home had left him reeling, even at that young age.

*Charity fraud.*

His father had been soliciting donations to line his pockets, while making the public think him the best kind of benefactor, with Katherine essentially the face of the whole operation.

Laurence been horrified at first. He'd had no respect for his father, but he'd thought actual crime far beyond his capacity. Once that feeling had passed, however, he'd been *pleased*.

Finally, a way to pay his father back for years of negligence and show the world exactly what kind of man he was!

It had been easy to focus on his parents and not on Katherine, until the mingled look of awe, fear and misery on her thin face had drawn him to her side at his parents' New Year's party. She'd aroused a strange protectiveness in him that

night, one he hadn't liked. Caring was dangerous, and a young man seeking to get *out*—and
scorch the earth behind him as he left—must not
care for anyone he might destroy in the process.

That night he'd held Katherine's trembling little hand in his and seen how innocent she was.
It had kept him up all night. He'd asked himself
how he could do this without subjecting her to
the scrutiny and embarrassment he knew his father was in for, keep her name from being connected to scandal for the rest of her life? How
could he get her out swiftly?

Warning her would do no good, he'd reasoned.
She'd never believe him over the people who had
given her everything for months. Katherine was
shy and softly spoken, tiptoeing round the house,
always with a book in her hand, and she absolutely idolized his mother. There was also the
chance she'd tell her parents about his plans to
expose them. No, he had to be merciless about it.

What was the absolute worst thing that Katherine could do that would make his image-con-
scious, hypocritical parents do away with her
*immediately*?

The day after the party Laurence had purchased a pair of lacy underwear, planted it at
the foot of his bed for the nosy maid to find, then

sat back and waited. When his parents had confronted him, he'd managed a guilty look, then smiled.

"It happened after the party," he'd lied. "We got drunk."

He cringed to think of it now. What a little snot he'd been—and so proud of his noble intentions. He'd been exposed to so many machinations as a child that they'd come as second nature to him once he was old enough to formulate manipulations of his own.

His father had held up a hand against his mother's angry hysterics, silencing her. He'd fixed ice-blue eyes on Laurence then, for a long moment, as if assessing his story.

"Is there a chance she is pregnant?" he'd asked.

Laurence's courage had left him at that point; he had shaken his head dumbly. It had been his intention to say there was, to up the threat of scandal, but there was something ugly, something dangerous in his father's eyes, that stopped him cold. He'd always thought himself a good judge of what his father was capable of, but at that moment he'd wondered.

His father's lip had twitched, as if Laurence had verified something he'd thought all along. "I'll take care of it."

He had—and swiftly. Katherine had been gone in less than a week, and to where Laurence had not cared. He'd soon been back at school in New England where, despite the cold, his hatred for his father had been able to blossom, grow, thrive. He'd leaked the information from his tiny dorm room, sat back and watched the internet implode.

Katherine had been safely out of the way. He remembered that her name hadn't come up in the fallout. Not *once*. But now what he'd done as a teenager was coming back to bite him— and hard.

Katherine had saved his life, true, but what had she been doing at the party in the first place? She'd recognized him and hadn't identified herself. She had no idea what he'd done for her. In her head, she likely thought he'd smeared her name maliciously.

It was well within Katherine's rights to return and exact revenge for what he'd done to her so long ago. Trouble was, he had no idea what she knew. Was her contact with him made out of anger, a determination to right a wrong? Or had she, perhaps, decided she would entice the Stone heir into giving her something? She'd already scammed a meal, crashed a party, and *kissed* him.

Was it an attempt to get something out of him? A way to taunt him? A warning? A seduction? How much did she *know?*

He felt his throat tighten at the memory of their encounter—along with another part of his body. Closing his eyes briefly did not help. All he saw was Katherine's body in sharp relief, her breasts undulating under that flimsy dress with every breath she took, her eyes cloudy from their kiss. She'd kissed him, yes, but he'd felt want as sharply as if he'd been the one to initiate it.

*Danger.*

"Laurence?"

He blinked and she came back into focus. She looked wary now. *Good.* He preferred it that way.

"Giles is a potential client," Laurence said shortly. "He was to meet my date this evening, and she was…indisposed."

He could tell from her face that she didn't believe a word of his lie. "Is her name Katherine as well?"

He did not answer the pointed question; the nuances were too much to explain. He breathed an inward sigh of relief when he saw one of the black Mercedes in his company's fleet approaching.

"I was coming down from my suite with a

very young and very disheveled woman next to me—"

She huffed. "*Young?* We're practically the same age."

He ignored her. "It doesn't look right. And looking *right* is everything in my line of work. Maintaining the charade costs you nothing, and I guarantee he won't remember you."

Hurt flashed across her face, but he ignored it. Katherine's feelings were not his concern—not when he had other things to worry about.

"Telling an outright lie and dragging a stranger into it didn't bother you at all?" Katherine pressed.

The irritation that had needled him at first grew into a full-on assault of his senses. He inhaled once to calm himself, then turned on her. Normally he would have left it alone, given himself time to plan what he would say and why he'd say it. However, there was something in her audacity that made him speak.

"I may have lied, but you sneaked *uninvited* into a private event—not to mention the charging your meal bit—to do who knows what. May I ask your motives, Katherine? Why me, and why *now*, after so many years?"

Her face blanched as his implication sank in.

* * *

Kitty's whole body was tightening, growing taut, as if in reaction to the proximity of his. It was a tightness that wound like a coiled spring...a tightness that needed release. At that moment she felt utterly miserable. She'd spent ten years freeing herself of the influence of people like the Stones, and with one look Laurence Stone had made her feel as if nothing had changed.

Instinctively she crossed her arms over her chest and his full mouth curved up into a smile. It was a half-smile—not one of sympathy, but of resentment. Suspicion.

"Answer me," he said, and his voice was cold. "You wouldn't be the first past acquaintance who thought they could grift off me."

Kitty felt penned in, crushed by the weight of his wordless accusations. Laurence's eyes were still on her, dark with that same odd anger and with something else—something that made her stiffen.

He looked...triumphant, almost. Vindicated. As if he'd been proved right. And that made something flare up in Kitty that had little to do with lust, or intimidation, or any of the myriad emotions that had been crushing her ribcage up till this point.

She lifted her chin, uttered a short, foul phrase that made him draw back with an expression of surprise. She felt pleased for the first time that evening.

"That," she spat out, "is none of your business, and my appearing in a *public* hotel had nothing to do with you. I can see that you're still a Stone, through and through. If you want to give me a ride, give me a ride. But I will not be interrogated like I'm one of your father's staffers!"

Laurence stared at her, unblinking, then looked away.

Kitty let out the breath she'd been holding. "The name of your firm is Laurence & Haddad," she pointed out. "I had no way of connecting it to you. I don't know anything about advertising."

"It isn't hard to Google."

But some of the animosity had left his face— he knew she was right, though she suspected he'd rather be crushed by that scaffolding than admit it. They stood in tense silence for a moment, then he spoke.

"Thank you for saving my life," he said.

It was a stiff concession, but he'd made it. Kitty felt some of the tension leak from her shoulders and risked a glance at him. He was staring straight ahead, a muscle working in his jaw.

"I will see that you are suitably rewarded."

"No need," Kitty said.

Anything that would prolong her contact with this insufferable man was something she had no interest in. Despite her body's reaction to him—which was wholly physical and born out of adrenaline, she told herself sternly—he would be the worst possible person to extend conversation of any kind with.

"Just do me one favor?"

He looked at her.

"Don't tell your parents you saw me."

His face grew even more cold and still, if that were possible. It was extraordinary, the way it varied from showing those quick flashes of emotion to complete immobility, as if he'd drawn down a blind.

"I haven't spoken to either one of them in ten years. You needn't worry on that account."

*Interesting.*

Kitty opened her mouth, but a Mercedes pulled up to the curb at that second and a driver scrambled out of the front seat, apologizing profusely.

"I'm sorry, sir. The whole place is blocked off and—"

"Not to worry. This is Miss Asare, Mason. Please take her to—"

"Astoria," Kitty said.

"Queens," Laurence said, his lip curling faintly, as if he smelled something off.

Kitty felt a new stab of anger, at him, for being so rude, and at herself, for the flash of embarrassment she'd felt. She was past being intimidated by people like this pompous *ass*.

"Katherine…" He hesitated. "I can't say that it's been lovely to see you again."

Kitty had never in her life rolled her eyes, but she did it now, stepping into the back of the luxury sedan. She saw a flash of amusement on Laurence's face as he bent to peer at her through the glass, lifted a hand to wave.

*Thank you*, he mouthed.

It was not until Kitty was home and stripping off her ruined finery that she realized she still had his tuxedo jacket, tucked around her shoulders as if it belonged there.

# CHAPTER SIX

KITTY FORCED HERSELF out of bed on Monday morning, feeling sluggish and dull. She switched off her alarm, stepped into the hottest shower she could stand, and was walking out the door in the next half-hour, her dress from Friday night wadded in a parcel under her arm. She'd have to mail it back today or they'd charge her already strained credit card for the full amount. She just hoped the dress wasn't so damaged they couldn't take it back.

Walking in her black high-tops over the grimy sidewalks of Astoria and navigating around vendors hawking everything from umbrellas to hand-painted silkscreens of the Empire State Building made the weekend's encounter seem all the more surreal.

Kitty quickened her steps, as if physical movement could help her outrun her thoughts. She lived in what her landlord trendily called a "community loft." In reality it was dormitory-style shared housing reminiscent of an old-fashioned boarding house.

Kitty had a small room, with basin, bed, chair, nightstand, and wardrobe, to herself. She shared an enormous bathroom with several other residents, as well as a massive kitchen and lounge. The best part of living there—and the reason she'd gone for it, other than price—was the fact that the two top floors had been converted into shared office space that was free to use for the residents. There Kitty worked in solitude, six days a week. She occasionally had a coffee or a night out with a few of the other residents, but no close friends, no permanent ties. She was hyper-focused on her work.

Kitty could have lived somewhere else if she'd wanted to—somewhere more appropriate for a twenty-seven-year-old business owner. However, this suited Kitty and her minimalist approach to life quite well. She didn't need anything other than reliable wi-fi and desk space. She didn't host, wasn't dating, and that meant she could funnel so much more of what she made into her foundation, One Step Ahead.

Laurence Stone and his opulent lifestyle, no matter how seductive both were, had no place in her everyday life. She needed to force him out of her headspace. Desperation had driven her to the event on Friday night. She had bills to pay, and chasing a check was the only way to get money quickly.

Although she kept her costs to a minimum, there were kids expecting their monthly allowances in only a few days. She'd just replaced her ancient laptop after it had given up the ghost two weeks before, and on-boarded two new clients at the same time. Thankfully her endowment would cover that, but she had other costs—her rent, what she ate, and her own salary, which had been more of a theory than a practicality since the beginning of the year.

Laurence Stone and his offer to pay her back for saving his life came back to her as she went over her accounts in her head, once, twice, three times, as if thinking about them again would change the balance. However, all thoughts stopped there: getting involved with Laurence never had been and never would be an option.

Kitty was so engrossed with her thoughts that she didn't see the sleek black E-Class until it caught up to her at an intersection. The back door opened and Laurence Stone peered out at her, looking incredulously at his surroundings.

"So this is Queens."

Kitty's jaw sagged downwards.

"Get in," he said.

Kitty took a very large step back.

Laurence had the gall to look irritated. "I need to talk to you. Come on. I'll take you wherever it is you're going."

*The hell you will!*

Kitty stared at him in disbelief, then turned and began walking in the other direction, back toward her building. Rapidly. If nothing else, there was a security guard called Rafe just inside the double doors, who'd had a thing for her since she moved in.

Laurence Stone, the psycho, she saw, had climbed out of the car, cupped his hands round his mouth, and was calling after her.

"You can do this now, or I can show up at your office! Your choice."

Kitty whirled around. "This is harassment," she spat out. "I can call the police, you know."

The look on his face was smug; he had never, she thought exasperatedly, looked more like his father.

"Call them. You can explain why you charged three hundred dollars' worth of food to my room Friday night."

*Oh!* What felt like most of the blood in her

body rushed directly to her face. "You—" she began.

"You can call me names later, Katherine. Just get in." His voice had resumed its usual dryness. "You were in my room for over an hour with no issues, so you can't be afraid I'll take advantage of you."

The light had changed and Laurence's car still sat in the middle of the intersection. His face was immovable as cars began to honk and creep round him, and drivers leaned out their windows, swearing colorfully.

The din frazzled Kitty completely. She let out a huff, then moved forward. "I am *not* getting in the car with you."

"You don't have to. Drive on, Mase," he added, and the car lurched into motion, making a U-turn that made Kitty gasp and easing smoothly into traffic.

"You never got back to me, you know," Laurence said mildly. "I was serious about giving you something."

"I don't want anything from you."

"At the moment. Is that it?" he said quietly.

Kitty found herself locked in his gaze. Although his skin was much lighter than hers, a fine bronze in contrast to her soft sienna undertones, his eyes were darker, and they gleamed. They were the type of eyes a girl could get lost in, were she not careful, and she'd already kissed him, she thought helplessly.

He was moving nearer her now, closing the distance between them as if the presence of the people on the street mattered little.

"We may have a problem that I need to discuss with you," he said.

*"We?"*

"I assure you that I'm as appalled as you are." His voice was clipped. "Thirty minutes of your time will suffice."

Kitty pursed her lips, then shrugged and pointed at her building. There were no coffee shops or restaurants on this strip of sidewalk. She had a moment's hesitation, thinking of Laurence coming into her humble space, but she forced it back, angrily. If it was good enough for her, it was certainly good enough for Laurence Stone, with his Mercedes-driven arrogance!

She began marching down the street without looking to see if he followed, then punched in her door code and entered, pausing to nod at Rafe. The grizzled guard looked curiously at Laurence, and even more curiously at his identification, but waved them through without any questions.

Laurence, as expected, was not well-bred enough to keep his comments to himself, and began talking as soon as they walked into the lounge. "You *live* here?"

"Were you expecting the Ritz-Carlton?"

Kitty stalked over to a couple of distressed leather chairs in her favorite corner of the communal lounge area. Luckily most of the residents of her building had gone to work, either upstairs or to their offices outside, and the place was virtually empty.

"You are unbearably spoiled," Kitty snapped, and lowered herself into the chair, dropping her parcel on the floor. "Say your piece. I've got to get to the post office."

Laurence looked at her measuringly and to her surprise broke out into a smile—a real one—that softened his face so dramatically she was taken completely off guard. The fluttering in her chest was equally discomfiting.

He dusted the leather with a handkerchief in a show that she suspected was for her benefit, then sat and extended his long legs.

"We've gone viral," he said.

When Kitty's brow furrowed with confusion he sighed.

"That means—"

"I know what it means!"

"Very well." He extracted a slim, top-of-the-line tablet from its carrying-case and laid it on the scratched Formica table between them. "Google away. I'm going to…" his lip curled slightly as he looked around "…visit the water dispenser. If one can call it that."

*Snob.* Kitty rolled her eyes and tapped away.

"Can I get you anything?"

"I don't need anything from you."

It was as if he hadn't heard her, or rather chosen not to listen.

"You have a vending machine in the corner," he said, "that seems to be selling *coffee.* I'm intrigued. Would they take American Express?"

"Why don't you go over there and see?"

He said something else before he ambled off, but Kitty tuned him out. Once she looked up Laurence's name and "The Park Hotel" hundreds of hits came up; the video, it seemed, was everywhere.

Some enterprising cellphone holder had recorded them, uploaded it to his personal account with a long thread ranting about safety. Views were gaining traction, mostly shared by indignant city-dwellers insisting that something be done about the never-ending construction in midtown, but something else had caught the attention of the public—Laurence's "rescue."

"*I* saved *your* life!" Kitty exclaimed in disbelief, scrolling past the comments.

Unfortunately no one had captured those first few moments, but had yanked out their phones when she was already on the ground and Laurence had tugged them to safety from the road. One image made her breath catch in her throat: she and Laurence, on the ground, him cradling her and looking down at her with an expression of tenderness that made her skin flush hot.

"Combined with the fact that I told Giles Mueller you were my girlfriend, it's made things slightly awkward," Laurence said, his dry voice breaking her concentration. He set down a paper cup of coffee in front of her. "This," he said, "tastes precisely as if someone has burned beans, soaked the pot in water, taken that water, added milk and sugar—"

Kitty didn't want to drink it—vending machine coffee was disgusting—but caffeine was exactly the boost she needed to clear her brain right now. She gulped, welcoming the scald at the roof of her mouth.

"I don't see how this is my problem," she said, flatly. "You have more to worry about than I do

if anyone makes the connection. I didn't do anything wrong."

"Didn't you?"

"No!"

How she hated that loftiness. It was as if he'd
placed himself on some sort of invisible pedestal,
from where he could look down and smirk and
wield that sardonic voice of his like a lash. He
thought he was better than her. They all thought
they were better than her. Kitty felt her anger
flare.

"Just get to it, Laurence—you bullied me into
letting you come here," she added. "What do
you want?"

*She's beautiful.* And her anger only heightened
it, brightened her eyes, illuminated her skin. The
thought surprised him.

They sat in silence for a moment, looking, he
thought fleetingly, like any other couple. They
could have been co-workers, lovers—or, hell,
just friends. Laurence could not remember the
last time he'd sat with a friend like this; those
meetings were restricted to days long past, in
high school and university—days when he'd still
cared about what people thought of him, when

he'd still been looking for the family he didn't have at home.

Those friends had proved as disappointing as his home life had been. No matter how long, how wild those nights were, his companions would inevitably go home, and he would be left alone.

*Home.* There never had been such a place for him. He'd have one eventually, when he was old and tired and needed somewhere to rest his head. For now, though, he worked and did his best to ensure he'd never need a penny of his father's inheritance. He would surpass it.

And partnering with Katherine Asare would add a significant chunk to his holdings.

Giles had already declared himself absolutely charmed by her—why, Laurence had no idea—but if he could get her to agree to this he'd not only have a stand-in for Aurelia, he'd be able to find out what had happened to Katherine—and, potentially, why she'd shown up. He still did not trust that their meeting had happened by coincidence, and Laurence knew that keeping a possible enemy close was the safest way to proceed.

Also, if Laurence was being honest with himself, there was a third reason that was far more elemental. Katherine was attractive, and he was not completely unmoved by occasional pleasures such as good whisky, good food, a soft, scented woman in his bed. It had been a long time since he'd had the third, and after the way she'd kissed him—

She was trying too hard to look unconcerned; he could feel the tension coming off her in waves. Not as much as when they were in his suite on Friday night, but very much there.

"You look so very different than you did when you lived with them," Laurence said after a moment.

"I must," Katherine said, and her voice grew just a fraction softer. "You didn't remember me."

*For heaven's sake.*

Laurence eyed her face. So here it was, the part where they would acknowledge their shared past. He recognized it as necessary if he was to strike this deal with her, but that didn't mean he had to like it.

"It's been a decade, at least," he said, crisply.

"Nine years and eight months," Katherine said quietly.

Over the years the thin schoolgirl's body had yielded to a softness that nudged the confines of her garments just enough to catch attention. Her enormous eyes, lined with makeup, tipped upward, heavily lashed; her lips were soft and full.

She wasn't beautiful, not by any means, but she was very attractive—and just uptight enough to make him want to see her unravel.

"Lovely," he admitted. "You're quite lovely."

"What do you *want*, Laurence?" she cried out. "I signed all the NDAs… I've never said a word about any of you. I *left*. What do you want from me?"

Despite all his suspicions, Laurence could not deny one thing: this was a woman in distress, and he was the cause of it. It took effort to focus back on the fact that she could not be trusted, and when he did he steeled his face, tilted his head.

"I'd like you," he said, "to extend the ruse that we started—"

"*We* started?"

"You didn't protest," Laurence pointed out. "It would be rather inconvenient to change the story now that we've become so conspicuous—"

"Is that my fault?"

"Would you stop interrupting?" Laurence frowned. He couldn't remember her being this argumentative in those days—hell, he didn't remember her speaking much at all then. "It will only be for a few weeks this summer, until my arrogance drives you to the point of dumping me as publicly as possible. In return, I will pay you handsomely—"

"I'm not interested in your money," she snapped.

"Don't be ridiculous." He kept his voice even. It was easy for Laurence to make his voice low, seductive, non-threatening; advertising was based on that, in a sense. "You wouldn't be living here if you didn't need money."

Katherine's back stiffened with pride. "I live here by *choice*, Laurence. Big fancy homes mean nothing to me. Any income I get goes to my foundation. I only keep what I need to live on— the rest goes to helping people."

"You're a *businesswoman*," he said, emphasizing the word. "A new businesswoman, at that."

"So what?"

He'd done his research before coming out that morning, and what he'd found had both surprised and impressed him. Two years ago Katherine had applied for and won two prestigious grants, in order to start a charity that provided financial support and housing for young people exiting the foster care system. One Step Ahead, it was called.

She had a good model, although her reach so far seemed small. A cursory glance at her DIY website featured the success stories of some of her clients, as well as a list of names of patrons. He'd recognized a couple by reputation.

"I looked. It's an amazing idea," he admitted.

She'd been forced to make a way for herself after being cast out into the world and she had focused on helping others. It was admirable, though he'd never have done it himself. Laurence gave generously to various charities, but he'd never been one to do the dirty work himself.

Katherine looked wary, although the expression in her brown eyes had softened a fraction at the praise. "Okay. So?"

Laurence almost laughed aloud. There was something he liked about her prickliness. In the world of advertising everything was based on a company's ability to make everything seem smooth, pleasant, seamless. Katherine's irritation felt fresh.

"I won't insult you by offering you actual money—you'd probably throw it in my face."

"That's accurate." She *did* smile then, probably at the prospect.

"We're in a ridiculous situation," he admitted, leaning back into the cheap imitation wood chair, "but I was trying to think on my feet. I didn't anticipate it would escalate into something like this."

"Well…"

She was faltering; there was an uncertainty in her eyes that hadn't been there before. Katherine couldn't hide the expression in her eyes any more than a child could, and he found himself holding his breath before he remembered that he was there on a mission.

"Let me help you," he said, and his voice was a low husk, heavy with the sort of reassurance that was intended to persuade.

"I don't need your help."

But he saw her swallow visibly.

"I've never needed your help or anyone else's."

"Let me be your partner, then." He didn't hesitate. "Everyone needs somebody."

He realized even as he uttered the words how wholly hypocritical they were. First of all he didn't need anyone, and never had, and secondly it was something his father might have said, to reel in an unsuspecting voter. The thought made him feel sick, although he couldn't show Katherine that.

"What happened to your date?" she asked a little unsteadily. "Isn't she over her *indisposition*?"

Oh. He'd nearly forgotten the excuse he'd used, and he decided in a split second to speak honestly. Katherine Asare was someone who cut through directly to the heart of things; he'd have an easier time with her if he didn't dissemble.

"She dumped me," he said blandly.

Katherine looked pleased for the first time since they'd spoken. "I can't imagine why."

He decided it was time to round up the conversation. If they wandered into the weeds he'd be in danger of losing control, and Katherine Asare and those enormous eyes were digging in places they had no right to dig. Someone like her, with insight into his past, had the potential to do a great deal of damage.

"I'll speak plainly." The way he should have in the beginning, before she had him ruminating.

"All right."

"I'm close to signing the man you met. Giles Mueller. He's the owner of the Mueller Racetrack."

She nodded.

"You know it?"

"It's out on Long Island. I attended an event close to it once."

He grunted. "The woman you filled in for on Friday is—*was*—my set date for several events over the next month. Since Giles already thinks you're her, I'd like you to step in. In exchange, I'll make a handsome donation to your charity—"

"Foundation."

"Whatever you like."

There was silence between them for a moment, and Katherine looked at him again. It made him uncomfortable at once. He knew she couldn't see into his mind, but there was something very perceptive about that look. She said nothing, and he continued talking to cover the silence.

"You see, Katherine, I owe you a debt." Laurence's voice was dry. "You saved my life, and in turn I'll save your business."

She snorted. "What makes you think my business needs saving?"

Laurence laughed incredulously. "You're a one-person operation. You don't even have an *office*. Your website is one of those ghastly pay-by-month templates, you live in a boarding house—"

"I don't need an office," Katherine said proudly. "I meet clients in restaurants and coffee shops. An office is an old-fashioned and completely unneeded expense. I'm not looking to make money off this, Laurence. I want to help people. Not everyone is like you."

Laurence chose not to pursue the insult; what

mattered was getting Katherine to sign. "As you like," he said dismissively, then reached for his phone. "My driver has the paperwork waiting in the car. I'll have him bring it round now—"

"No."

It took a moment for the word to register. "Excuse me?"

Katherine did not repeat herself, but she did shake her head. "It's a kind offer, Laurence," she said firmly, "but the thought of playing your girlfriend is at least as absurd as your lie was."

Laurence realized after several seconds had passed that he was gaping, and he closed his mouth rapidly. He'd anticipated many different counteroffers—all that had been provided for in the partnership proposal that was ready for her to sign—but a refusal was something he was wholly unprepared for.

"You're saying no?" he said, to clarify.

She nodded.

"Why the hell would you say no?" The question came out far more harshly than he would have liked, but he was genuinely shocked. "You have everything to gain."

She tucked a lock of dark hair behind her ear, and he was momentarily distracted by the smooth slide of it over her skin. The change in her was truly remarkable. In her element, she was an entirely different person than the frightened teenager he remembered, and she carried herself with a quiet dignity that was very attractive.

"Besides our shared past, which I'm keen to keep there," she said, "I don't want a donation based on a bribe. It's unethical."

"So is soliciting money by crashing other people's events."

She had the grace to look embarrassed at that jibe, though she sat proud and tall. "I stand by what I said."

Silence reigned for a moment and Laurence stared over Katherine's head, trying to think. How could he make the absurd girl cooperate? Inwardly, he felt some admiration for her integrity, but not enough to let her go without getting what he wanted.

He was silent for so long that she began to squirm.

"Are we done here, Laurence?"

He ignored the question. "Indulge me," he said, "by telling me again what you were doing at my party."

Her lips compressed. "One of your guests promised me a donation, and I was hoping…" She faltered for the first time.

"That running into her at a social event would be a good reminder?"

She looked embarrassed, but that defiance was still on her face. "Social events are where the people I need are, Laurence. I go to as many as possible, to network and meet people."

"Huh…" An idea was forming in Laurence's head. "And you won't take money from me?"

"No, I won't."

Her lower lip was thrust out. The petulant gesture only brought attention to how full and soft it was, although he supposed she'd be horrified to know his thoughts were wandering in that direction.

"Let's say you agree to do this—no, no, I'm just speaking rhetorically," he added, waving a hand for her to be quiet. "The first event we'd go to is the opening day of races for the summer season at the Mueller Racetrack. I don't recall the entire guest list, but the Regevs, the Davises and the Van Cortlandts will be there, in Mueller's box. It'd be a wonderful opportunity, Katherine…there on the arm of your *devastatingly* handsome escort—"

"Don't make me sick."

She was thinking, though. He could see it in her eyes. She frowned, a myriad of emotions flitting across her lovely face.

"Introductions. From me to every single one. And no need to crash. Your name will be on all the table settings. Maybe even a gift bag to take home," Laurence added. "I'd make sure you met everyone, of course, and talk up your charity—"

"Foundation."

"Foundation, and don't interrupt me. We'll get a new website up by the time we attend—yours is an amateur disgrace—and you'll have more donations than you know what to do with. In upcoming weeks I'll be hosting a dinner for the Muellers and several other clients of mine, to welcome them to the family—"

"Isn't that a little presumptuous, given you haven't signed them yet?"

"Oh, I'll sign them. There'll be golfing, and dinners, and late drinks, and Broadway shows— all the usual song and dance we do to make clients more amiable. You'll make a *killing*."

Katherine was chewing her lip, releasing its plump softness and drawing it back again in the most distracting way. He wanted to run his thumb over it, see if the touch would make her inhale the way she had the first time they'd kissed.

"You'll keep your hands to yourself," she said after a pause.

Laurence almost laughed aloud; it was as if she'd read his mind. Was that what she was most worried about?

"Are you asking me or telling me? I'll do as much as is needed to make it believable," he conceded.

"Connections?" she said, as if she were trying to convince herself.

"Connections. That's it. No money. I won't even make a donation."

"And I'll have to play your girlfriend for…?"

"A month. Six weeks, tops. I'll even let you plan your exit. Throw wine in my face in a public place, if you'd like."

She was trying not to smile now, at the thought of that. A glitter was coming into her brown eyes and Laurence found it sparked a warmth inside him that had little to do with lust.

"Well…?" he drawled.

She swallowed, then quickly put her hand across the table. He took it. He wanted to whoop in triumph, but he quelled the impulse—as well as the thought that perhaps he was more excited at the prospect of spending time with Katherine Asare than he should be. After all, would it be so hard just to say to Giles that he'd been dumped?

He pushed the thought aside, focused on her instead. "It's a deal, Katherine."

"No. Not yet." She shook her head so vigorously that her hair brushed her cheeks. "One condition—besides all the others I haven't thought of yet. Your parents can't know about this."

Laurence inhaled sharply. *His parents.* The reason they'd met in the first place, and a sore subject for both of them. "I don't talk to either of them—"

"Promise me!"

"You have my word that I won't tell them. The media…that's a little more out of my control. But I will take every precaution." That, at least, he knew he'd be able to do.

Katherine nodded stiffly, then stood. "I have to go to the post office," she said. "And, no, I don't want a ride, so don't offer."

"Shouldn't the guy you're dating—?"

"Don't push it, Laurence."

He nodded, trying to keep the satisfaction from his face. Katherine didn't respond well to smugness. "Shall we meet at my office when you're free this week? Discuss particulars?"

"Fine."

"I'll send you the address—"

"No. I'm sure I can find it," she said dryly. "Goodbye, Laurence Stone."

# CHAPTER SEVEN

THE FIRM OF Laurence & Haddad was housed in a predictably tall, angular glass building. Not on Madison Avenue, as Kitty had expected—obviously too many viewings of *Mad Men*—but a bit further away, tucked discreetly at the end of a street not too far from Grand Central Station.

Safe in the privacy of her room, Kitty had agonized over what to wear to her lunch meeting with that cool, worldly creature and had finally settled on a black Chanel dress with a short, pleated skirt. It was one of the last things Mrs. Stone had given her before she'd left them, and the only designer dress in her closet that wasn't thrifted. Kitty no longer bought new clothes on principle.

"Every girl needs a little black dress, and you're eighteen soon," the woman had said breezily as she'd towed a seventeen-year-old Kitty through Barney's.

The former supermodel hadn't had the foresight to think about how impractical a wardrobe such as she'd given her would be, Kitty guessed, and most of it had gone to consignment shops, piece by piece, over the years. She'd kept the Chanel dress, though, almost as a charm—for good luck or bad, she could not say.

Ten years later Mrs. Stone's fashion advice had held up—the dress looked as in style as it had the day she'd bought it. Thank God it still zipped, skimming and clinging to Kitty's subtle curves and showcasing her long slim legs. It made everything come full circle, in a sort of bizarre way.

A rush of cool, scented air hit her when she walked through the revolving door, and a petite blonde woman with hair trimmed into a pixie cut appeared in front of her.

"Miss Asare?" She pronounced Kitty's name perfectly. "I'm Cordelia. Please follow me."

Kitty was glad she wore flats; Cordelia's gait was unforgiving. She hustled Kitty into one of the elevators that seemed to swoop down and open, magically, at her behest, but did not initiate any more conversation, just typed busily away at her phone with a sleek black stylus.

When they reached their destination they entered a foyer that was bustling with activity.

Glass-walled offices lined the corridors, and Kitty could see people inside with computers, whiteboards, monitors, artwork on easels. Advertisements in sleek black frames lined the walls, many of which she recognized. It was mostly fine alcohol, jewelry, one very tiny foreign car. Decadent in a way she definitely couldn't afford—and yet it was refined. Sophisticated. Carefully curated.

All the things that Laurence Stone was.

Cordelia steered Kitty efficiently down the center hallway. She waved her keycard in front of one door, punched buttons on another, pushed open a third, and then—

It was as if they'd entered another world. The suite was quiet and cool, full of sunlight pouring in from ceiling-to-floor-length windows and skylights. Water ran over white and pale blush-colored pebbles in a reflection pool sunk into the floor, elegant furniture rendered in whites and creams decorated the space.

"This is Mr. Stone's private wing. We're going to be in conference room one," Cordelia said, and opened yet another door.

Kitty blinked, clutching her handbag tight to her side. The conference room was decorated much like the receiving room, except for the long white marble-covered table that ran down the center. It was covered by an assortment of dishes covered in filigreed bone-white covers, from which all sorts of savory smells emitted. At the head of the table stood Laurence Stone, looking a whole different type of formal in a sleek charcoal-gray suit and a black shirt that set off the smooth tints of his skin so vividly he seemed to glow.

His face was still. He looked nothing like the dry, exasperatingly amused man she'd shared an hour with in the office at her building earlier that week. He looked as if he could put a kill order out on someone and lie effortlessly about it—or at the very least smash a girl's heart to bits. She was glad to see him this way. It would be an apt reminder of who he was.

"Katherine," he said.

And there it was—that odd little twist of the consonants in her name. Her stomach responded with a flip.

"Laurence," she replied, after swallowing hard.

Laurence jerked his head in Cordelia's direction. "You may leave us."

She turned on her heel and left.

Laurence smiled, but the motion didn't reach his eyes. Kitty was struck by how much he resembled the Senator in this environment, with that look on his face.

"I thought lunch in the office would be nice," he said simply. "Please sit down."

Kitty did so and he followed. A man dressed all in black materialized from the background to fill water glasses and lift the lids off the dishes. There was a beautifully roasted chicken, mashed potatoes, fresh vegetables, a bright beet salad, and lemon pie with piles of whipped cream to finish it off.

"You probably would have preferred a restaurant, but the food is quite good here," Laurence said easily, carving the bird with unexpected skill. "White, dark…?"

She swallowed, determined not to appear intimidated. "A leg."

Laurence draped a linen napkin over her lap and filled her plate before attending to his own and sitting down. The china was plain, but thin and gleaming; the silverware was heavy and polished to a high shine. All very good quality.

She took her first bite of chicken and sighed appreciatively. Fork-tender and seasoned to perfection.

"Good?"

"Wonderful," she admitted guardedly, and then

paused to load her fork with the potatoes, creamy and golden with butter.

"Well, I know you only eat the best, so..."

Kitty's fork clattered down to her plate. "Are you *ever* going to stop alluding to that?"

"Not until the day I die."

"You probably would never have noticed," Kitty huffed. "And I knew anyone in the penthouse suite wasn't going to be financially ruined by a couple of glasses of wine."

"It was stupid." Laurence leaned back, clearly enjoying Kitty's discomfort.

"Well, I'm not sorry," Kitty said irritably. "And if you mention it again I'm not going to speak to you."

"Our first quarrel!"

Kitty leaned forward indignantly, but he spoke again.

"Don't be so sensitive. It only gets in the way of success. Look," he said, leaning in so those piercing eyes were squarely fixed on her face, "I meant what I said. I want to help you."

"You mean, you want to help yourself." Kitty attempted to calm the churning of her stomach by taking a long sip of mineral water. "Your father was the same way."

Laurence's hand came down hard on the table-top and Kitty nearly leapt out of her skin. He did not shout, but his voice gave her chills.

"Listen. We won't be together for long, but while we are you will not speak of the Senator to me. Not now, not *ever*."

"Why? I'm sure he wouldn't approve of this little agreement…" She could practically feel the rage emitting from his pores, but she couldn't have stopped even if she wanted to. "After all, he threw me out."

Laurence stared at her as if he was trying to choose between shaking her or tossing her out as his father had. He settled for leaning back in his chair, and then spoke through a jaw as rigid as the marble top of the conference table.

"My father was expert at using people, Kitty. I'm sorry he did it to you."

*I'm sorry he did it to you.*

She did not trust Laurence; she would *never* trust him. Their shared past was enough to ensure that. He'd been kind to her once, but he was one of *them*. It would be foolish to forget that.

Kitty cleared her throat, and when she spoke there was much less animosity in her voice, though it was still guarded. "How did you get into advertising?"

"I got into the business with a schoolmate of

mine, years ago—he runs the international side of things and I handle North America."

"Desmond Haddad?" Kitty said, remembering the second name on the door.

"The very one." Laurence seemed uninterested in talking about his business partner. "How'd you get into philanthropy?"

She took a breath and picked up her fork again, allowing herself to be seduced into complacency by the food, which really was excellent.

"I worked as a grant writer for a non-profit for a few years, and went solo a couple of years ago. I've been able to help about ten kids," she said, and she could not stop the pride from coloring her voice.

A man like Laurence Stone would have no idea what it meant to be able to offer stability and security to a young person who had nobody, but having the rug pulled out from under her at such a young age herself had left her with a near obsession with helping people in the same situation.

Laurence smiled, and Kitty fought the little flip in her stomach with all her strength. He was *ridiculously* attractive. More so than any man had the right to be.

Kitty was no stranger to attraction, but her life left little room for romance. Men, in her limited experience, were selfish creatures; everything they gave was tied to ego. The Senator had taken her in because it had made him look good. Men in college had approached her because she'd blossomed, gained new confidence, made *them* look good. It was dangerous to engage with men unless you were in a position where you needed absolutely nothing from them.

After all, her reliance on the Stones had caused her devastation, and even as a young girl she'd sworn she'd never allow herself to be in that position again. She could not allow Laurence Stone to run roughshod over her inner vows, no matter how warm his lips were, or how she wondered exactly what the hint of shadow she could see on his jaw might feel like on her bare skin...

"Very commendable," was all he said.

She stood, pushed back her chair, and took a full step back. He smiled—much to her discomfort. There must be something truly wrong with her, Kitty thought with some despair, that she reacted so primally whenever he was near.

She closed her eyes in order to shut him out, heard rather than saw him stand up, come closer to her.

"Are you all right?"

She nodded. "Just wanted to..." She could

come up with no viable excuse, and instead chose to ignore the question. "Thank you for lunch."

"You didn't eat much."

No, and what she'd eaten was now knotted in her stomach. She placed a hand on her abdomen. "If this is going to work, I guess you should call me Kitty."

"What?"

"My friends started calling me that at university."

It had matched the new persona she'd taken on there—confident, strong, and outrageously independent, with a hint of sauciness that manifested in her attitude, her bold makeup, her graceful swaying-hipped walk. She felt none of those things, now; she felt a little like a fraud. Laurence had seen her when she was less than nothing, and she wondered now if these superficial gains meant anything to him.

"Kitty. It suits you." He paused, as if to savor the name on his tongue, then continued. "I plan on taking very good care of you during our time together."

His deep voice curved round the words, taking them from something innocent to something else entirely…something that tightened her stomach, eased down to her loins.

"Kitty, look at me," he commanded, although it didn't sound at all like a command. It was gentle, soft, with a hint of tenderness that drew her like a moth to flame. She'd always been a fool for a kind word.

She opened her eyes.

Thankfully, Laurence wasn't looking at her; he was looking at her hand, at the balled fist she'd made. He reached out, and before Kitty could stop him he took her wrist in between his fingers.

"You're bruised," he observed, and a lump rose in Kitty's throat.

One of the injuries she'd sustained that night was a bruise just above her pulse-point; it had darkened to a very nice shade of purple just yesterday. It faded for the most part into her dark skin, but was still visible to a sharp eye.

"Can I take a look?" he asked, gently.

Kitty felt heat take over her body as palpably as it had that night. It was as if every cell of arousal she had was primed to react to Laurence Stone's touch, though her brain knew it was the worst idea she could possibly hope to have. He was touching her wrist, and barely that, and her body was reacting as strongly as if she were naked beneath his gaze. She felt a familiar tingle…one that would crest and reduce to an ache. She knew without looking down that her nipples would have swelled, puckering as if for his mouth.

"Fate brought us together for a reason," he said simply.

Laurence was still stroking her skin almost absentmindedly, much as he'd done that New Year's night. Kitty should snatch her hand away, but—

*You don't want to.*

That thought was enough for Kitty to yank her hand back—that and the fact that she was breathing as heavily as if she'd run up a flight of stairs to get here. She licked her lips, fighting for composure. The room felt smaller, smelled far too male. And Laurence—

Laurence Stone was smiling. He knew. He *knew.* And he was using that weakness against her—wielding it above her head like a weapon.

It was precisely, she thought, what his father might do.

Kitty shifted on trembling legs, pressed her thighs together beneath her brief skirt. The ache there now was delicious. The type of ache produced by lust and assuaged only by the type of roughness a man of his size and strength would be able to offer.

"Kitty…" His voice was strangely gentle.

"No. I'm not interested in—"

Was it normal, the fact that her chest was rising and falling so rapidly? She willed herself to calm, for her blood pressure to lower, for the heat that she knew flushed her skin to reduce. And the worst part—the absolute worst part of this—was…

*It isn't affecting him at all.*

There was no flush beneath that stunning copper skin, no uneasiness in his expression. All she saw was that immovable face, those stony eyes, and suddenly she felt a wave of helplessness wash over her.

Men like this, she thought, would always do what they willed. Get what they willed. The world was set up for them, and there wasn't a damned thing she could do about it.

She closed her eyes again. She could feel him getting closer, feel heat and warmth and smell spice and soap and other overwhelmingly good things. She didn't open her eyes…not even when she felt the warmth of his hand on the skin of her cheek.

"Kitty," he said, and his voice was almost kind.

"Believe it or not, my goal this afternoon is not to distress you. Please, look at me."

Kitty forced her eyes open, trying her best to ignore the headache forming behind her lids. Laurence was closer than he'd been that night in his hotel room, his full mouth pulled down a little at the corners this time, hovering tantalizingly above hers.

*Close enough to kiss*, Kitty thought, and a sigh escaped her lips.

It was as if her mind had magic powers, or some sort of magnetic force, because Laurence wasn't looking as enigmatic as he had been just seconds ago, and his slow, hot lips were nearly brushing hers, ever so softly, and she felt decidedly, certainly, as if she were going to die if he didn't.

*Kiss me.*

Laurence hadn't intended this—not at all. But, by God, now that he was kissing her he was glad he'd given in to impulse.

Kitty's mouth was plush and rich and sweet, like some fruit he'd never yet had the pleasure of tasting. He only brushed her lips with his at first, giving her the room to push him away if she wanted to, but she stiffened, then melted back against the cool hard surface behind her, letting out an exquisitely soft sound that made his blood surge in response, pooling downwards.

He kissed her with a gentleness he hadn't known he possessed until this moment. This was no plundering; it was an exploration. Kitty's body had softened beneath his as it had done that hazy night in his hotel room, a tantalizing hint at what she might be like were she ever to be naked and pliant in his arms.

When it ended, she looked up at him with kiss-swollen lips. "This isn't right," she whispered.

"No," he agreed.

But he did not let that observation prevent him from running a thumb over the silken length of her lower lip… part of her that he was virtually obsessed with at this point. He had not forgotten how deliciously plump it had become at his ministrations both then and now.

She closed her eyes for a moment, as if to shut him out, and he found suddenly that he didn't want that. He wanted to see what was written in those eyes, what he knew she would be too proud, too angry, to say.

A flash of panic crossed her thin face when he pulled back to look at it, and Laurence suddenly felt regret. Panic was decidedly not the emotion he wanted to elicit from this woman—especially not when he had her in such a vulnerable position.

Though his body cried out with frustration, he dropped his hands, somehow restrained himself from gripping her hips in his palms, and took a full step back.

She crossed her arms over her breasts. "I think we need to set out some ground rules."

He lifted a brow.

"If *this*..." she gestured at both of them "...is going to be a problem—"

The only problem he had was that he wanted to lock the door and finish what he'd started, but he doubted that revelation would be useful at this juncture.

"It won't," he said quickly.

"Are you sure?"

"Let's just say I've fulfilled my curiosity."

Her eyes clouded with shock and hurt, but he kept going. Harsh, he knew, but better. Were Kitty Asare a different kind of woman he might initiate an encounter—dirty, hot, fast. He'd done it before. However, Kitty's awkwardness indicated one thing: an innocence he had no interest in removing. He did not know if she'd had lovers before, or how many, but he would not make it his business, no matter how much his body cried out for it.

He cleared his throat. "Perhaps we should have a glass of water, and then I'll call Cordelia in while I bring you up to speed, yes?"

"Fine," she said between her teeth.

She'd turned her head to hide her face and Laurence suddenly felt an odd protectiveness—and something much more profound, much more uncomfortable.

*Guilt.*

The return of Kitty Asare into his life had presented Laurence with something he'd never had to deal with before: the consequences of his actions as an angry teenager, noble as his intentions might have been. He had a debt to pay—and, despite his millions, he wasn't sure he could afford the expense that wanting her would bring.

# CHAPTER EIGHT

LAURENCE WAS RIGHT about one thing: her association with him did produce results. Even though she hadn't yet gone on a single public date with the man, word had gotten out. Her website had crashed from the volume of visits, and funds had come pouring in with alarming speed.

Kitty was astonished at how thoroughly a few hundred thousand dollars could completely change the trajectory of someone's life in only a matter of hours.

Life as the girlfriend of Laurence Stone was changing Kitty's look, as well. The day after their office lunch Kitty was approached in her neighborhood again, this time by Cordelia, who ferried her to a four-hour appointment with a stylist in Soho. Her hair was conditioned, cut, blown out; extensions were put in, then cut; her eyebrows were threaded.

When she protested the cost, because she was

determined not to owe Laurence a penny for any of this, Cordelia had an answer ready.

"The girls who worked on you today are in training," she said briskly, "and the firm did an ad campaign for the salon's Paris location last year. Mr. Stone won't be paying a penny for this."

Kitty was suspicious, but she gave in—with very bad grace. She did recognize that looking the part was necessary, and that styling her thick locks herself always took more time than she liked...

Clothes were next. No arguments, Cordelia said. She would have a new wardrobe, and it would be supplied by Tania Lee—a wardrobe mistress who worked out of LA for a film company that Laurence & Haddad had done yet *another* campaign for.

"Laurence wishes you to appear successful," was Cordelia's explanation, after the delivery of a number of devastatingly chic designer outfits and boxes of jewelry marked for different occasions to Kitty's building.

It could, she supposed, be interpreted in several unflattering ways, but she closed her mouth against her response. Her fight wasn't with Cordelia.

"Again, no expense, Miss Asare," Cordelia

continued. "These are completely recycled from Tania Lee's film closet. Same with the jewelry—and it's all insured. Mr. Stone will have no arguments."

*No arguments? That arrogant son of a bitch.*

Kitty was fuming. She planned to tell Laurence exactly what she thought of him, as soon as she could get him alone. And she'd have that opportunity on her debut as Laurence's girlfriend: a day at the races, to take a look at Giles Mueller's racetrack.

On the day of the races Kitty was presented to Laurence by Cordelia at the door of his office, coiffed, dressed, made up, and ready to depart.

He looked up, surprised. "It's time already?"

"Yes, Mr. Stone. Chopper's ready."

Laurence sighed, gave his desktop one last longing look, and stood. He was wearing slim-cut trousers and a matching jacket of thin Italian wool, in the gray that Cordelia had mentioned was part of the "Ascot theme," with braces and a snowy white shirt. When she set eyes on him all the complaints she'd prepared flew out of her head, and she was suddenly glad she'd agreed to dress up.

Cordelia had her tablet poised. "Do you need anything else, sir?"

"Not a thing. Thank you, Cordelia."

When his assistant scurried away, Laurence looked Kitty over from head to toe, taking in the soft floral dress with the neckline that dipped demurely between her breasts, her small belted waist, her wax-smooth bare legs, the pointy-toed slingbacks that were so high she threatened to tip forward.

His eyes then climbed up, and his mouth twitched.

"Cordelia said I *had* to wear a hat," Kitty said defensively.

"It's very fetching."

Kitty had no time to process whether she'd been insulted or not, for he was steering her down the hall at a good clip.

Laurence's opinion of her designer pillbox aside, Kitty could not help but preen a bit. The high-shine chrome and mirror decor in his offices gave her prime opportunities to look at herself, and—well, Kitty really did love to dress up, with a girlishness that hadn't evaporated with all the realities of life.

It was like a montage in a fun but slightly problematic romantic comedy—being ushered into boutiques with names far too French for everyday wear and being dressed by a rich man's assistant. She knew she looked well. The creamy floral dress accentuated her slim waist and long legs, and her skin glowed with health against the pale fabric. She'd never seen anything so delicate before. It was from a period film set in the thirties, Cordelia had told her, and it was like wearing a watercolor...all soft swirls of gray and white.

The elevator took them all the way to the roof of Laurence & Haddad, where an enormous white and silver helicopter waited, blades circling madly. Kitty had a little trouble with her skirt, but somehow managed to cross the concrete without flashing anyone.

Laurence ascended without looking back, then turned to squint when he realized she hadn't yet quite made it in. "What in heaven's name are you doing?"

"I'm wearing heels!" She got in at last and arranged herself, a little breathless, into the nearest seat.

"Towel, ma'am?"

A woman in black trousers and a matching button-down approached Kitty with a smile. Laurence waved her away, but Kitty took the proffered towel, inhaled lavender and vanilla, and looked round the interior of the—was it called a *cabin* in a helicopter?

There were oversize reclining seats rendered in a buttery tan, meters of walnut paneling, in-flight entertainment, and the attendant, whose sole occupation seemed to be to make sure the half-hour or so it would take to get to Long Island would be spent in unwavering comfort.

"Is this the Senator's?" Kitty asked, wiping her hands and dropping the towel into the waiting basket.

Laurence did not react to her mention of his father the way he had the other day. In contrast, he seemed almost bored. "No, it's Desmond's."

"How nice of him to let you borrow it."

Laurence's brows drew together. "I can't maintain a helicopter as well as a yacht and a private plane, Kitty," he said, patiently. "It's excessive. You live in shared housing. I share a helicopter."

Kitty surprised herself by laughing out loud.

Laurence smiled. "I fold. I do have one, but it's out for repairs," he admitted. "I'm trying to think of what we would have had while you lived with us," he said thoughtfully. "Did they ever take you up in the chopper?"

Kitty shook her head, then stopped mid-motion

as her hat was already hanging on rather precariously. "No. It was an election year. Your mother said that you kept a low profile during those times."

Laurence's face darkened a bit. "Indeed."

"Please buckle in, ma'am," the attendant said from her seat next to the pilot, and then drew a privacy curtain.

By the time she'd attended to her belt Laurence had switched on a paper-thin tablet—one like she'd never seen in any store. Likely custom made for him, as everything else was.

Kitty crossed her legs and peered out of the window, watching as the chopper hauled itself skyward and the city began to fade behind them. She shot little glances at Laurence, but he didn't look up. She sighed, then allowed the pillowy softness of the seat to absorb her back, her hips.

So far, this was the quietest date she'd ever been on.

Despite his best efforts, he couldn't stop stealing glances at her.

Kitty looked remarkably like one of the vintage advertisements that Laurence had often gone back to for inspiration over the years, featuring a woman lounging at an airport in Havana. Like

Kitty, the woman was willowy and dark-haired, with the same chestnut skin and brilliant eyes, and she wore the same look of longing…of unfulfilled desire.

What did Kitty desire—and why did he care so much? She was his father's former foster child. He'd shared two kisses with her that crept into his memory at the most inappropriate times. She'd made him, for the first time in years, relive the most tumultuous period in his life. And now she was clearly discomfited by the way he was staring at her.

He didn't stop.

"Is there something on my face?" she blurted out.

"No."

She ran a self-conscious finger under both eyes anyway, then cleared her throat. "Are we just going to sit here and not talk until we get there?"

He lifted his shoulders. "Up to you—although you're remarkably bad at making conversation for someone who runs a charity."

Her eyes narrowed as she registered the insult. He did not have time to enjoy it, however, for she rallied back. "Fine. We'll talk."

"Do your best, sweetheart."

"What happened to you?" she asked. "After I left, I mean?"

Laurence blanched. He hadn't been expecting that line of conversation, that was for sure. "I'm sure an internet search would fill in those details."

She ignored that. "It was all over the news. You attempted to throw your father's election—"

He was ready for it this time. "That's a little extreme, Kitty. It was just a couple of social media posts."

"You accused him of fraud!"

Laurence put his tablet aside. To answer Kitty, he needed to focus. He had no intention of letting Kitty know exactly why she'd left the Stones' house, or his role in it; he still needed the Muellers to sign, and didn't know how she would react to that kind of information. A break with her now would only disrupt his plans.

"I was a horror," he said, careful to keep his expression neutral. "But I was a *boy*. I wanted attention; I didn't get it. Oldest story in the book."

He had to tread carefully here. He'd tell her just enough of the story to throw her off the scent... leave her role in it out completely.

"My father was a bit lax when it came to reporting his taxes accurately." He paused. "Some gumshoe at the *Times* thought he was living a little…*lavishly* for a public servant, and called for him to release his tax information, which he'd locked down tighter than the Vatican."

Kitty's eyes, which had been round with curiosity, blinked. "What does the Vatican have to do with—?"

"Nothing, it was a metaph— Stop interrupting, will you?" Laurence gathered his train of thought. "Anyway. I thought a good way to get dear Daddy's attention would be to leak the pages the fellow wanted, so I did. You can imagine the unpleasantness that followed."

*There.* That should be enough to satisfy her.

He could see Kitty wavering between curiosity and tact; unhappily, curiosity won.

"So you were sent away?" she asked.

"Something like that." Laurence picked up his tablet, signaling the end of the conversation. *Sent away* was definitely an understatement of the hell his father had put him through in retaliation for his disloyalty, but that wasn't Kitty's business—or something he was interested in reliving at the moment.

"I'm sorry that happened to you," she said, after a beat.

He shrugged his big shoulders. "I'm not. If

anything, it got me off my ass and made me work for everything I've got now. You did the same."

She was silent for a moment.

"We aren't the same," she said finally, and he had to look up, lean in to hear her over the blades of the chopper, the humming engine.

At that veiled accusation Laurence felt the first stirrings of defensiveness; he fought them down.

"Yes. You're far nobler," he said, dryly, wishing to God the girl wouldn't sit there, looking at him as if she pitied him.

No one pitied Laurence Stone; it simply wasn't a possibility. If anyone should be pitied, it should be Kitty. Yes, she'd been lucky to get out from beneath his father's machinations, but he was in her debt for the way he'd done it. He would pay it, he vowed inwardly. He would handle her business as if it were his own, introduce her to networks of people who would transform her financially. He'd ensure it succeeded if he had to front the whole damn thing himself.

Then Kitty Asare would finally be out of his life forever, and he could truly, completely, put their shared past behind him.

Laurence hated horse-racing, though he pretended not to. Nothing could interest him less than watching the sweating beasts gallop round the track, frothing at the mouth while veritable fortunes were made and lost in the stands.

The Mueller Racetrack was tucked into a heavily wooded part of the East End of Long Island. Unlike other tracks—Saratoga and Belmont—only certain types of horse-racing aficionados knew anything about it. The track was frightfully exclusive, and until last year had been completely private. Now that more people frequented the ground every year, for the invitation-only events Giles hosted, he'd gotten vetted by the New York Racing Association, and he needed Laurence's agency to present the track to the world in the most attractive light.

Today they'd greet the Muellers and do the type of schmoozing that he hated but was so necessary in his line of business. They would tour the track, pretend to like it, have a few drinks, take a few pictures. Then he'd be airlifted back to civilization faster than you could say Triple Crown.

They alighted from the helicopter and headed toward the main racetrack at an easy pace. Laurence kept a hand resting lightly at the small of Kitty's back, ostensibly to prevent her from swaying in her heels. He and Kitty rather stood out rather vividly; most of the crowd was as middle-aged and WASPY as his father, and all were eager to greet what Giles called "such an exotic couple."

"You look so familiar dear," Doris said upon introduction, squinting up at Kitty's face through her oversize sunglasses.

Kitty opened her mouth to reply, but Laurence cut in, placing a warning hand on her arm. "Kitty and I have been dating for a few weeks."

"Why, Laurence!"

"I know. It's very new, and I'm very fortunate."

Kitty looked as if she wanted to pass out, and he continued before she could speak. She'd have to work on not looking so horrified at the prospect of dating him if this was going to work.

"She runs a charitable foundation and has been kind enough to let me work with her on expanding her business," Laurence said, then on impulse squeezed her waist. She jumped a little, but she managed not to flinch—*just*. "Kitty provides incredible opportunities for young people in the system."

"Well, well… How lovely." The woman beamed. "It's so very important to give back to the community."

"Absolutely." Laurence tilted his head, taking on the diffident, modest tone he took when speaking to a potential client.

He launched into an abbreviated version of Kitty's story—her personal experience in the care system, her success story, her desire to give back. By the time he was finished Doris was shaking her head in amazement, a hand pressed to her bosom, and Giles was nodding gravely. He actually *clapped.*

"You are an extraordinary young lady, Kitty. Well done."

Kitty had a sour look on her face; perhaps her feet hurt. "I'm very pleased to meet you," she said finally.

"We're pleased to meet you as well! Will you join us in the box? First race is about to start," Doris said, sounding brisker.

She must be thinking about whatever thoroughbred she had her money on, thought Laurence.

"We'd love to." Laurence allowed his hand to slip to Kitty's hip. "Just lead the way."

*Of all the overbearing, conceited, self-important—!*

Kitty's anger had begun to mount when Laurence had cut her off so arrogantly. Kitty had no shame over her upbringing—it was no fault of hers, after all. However, the last thing she wanted was to be presented the way Laurence had just done. As a victim. As someone to be pitied—someone who only belonged in these circles because it would do her some good. It was the height of arrogance, of entitlement, and Laurence had proved to be no better than his sire!

His handsomeness, she reminded herself, was just a mask on the rottenness within. He'd always find some way to touch what she cherished, cover it with his dirty fingerprints, make it all about himself…

She pried his hand off her hip with as much force as she could—she didn't give a damn that they were in public. "Hold on," she said between her teeth, forcing him to come to a stop.

Oh, if he lifted his eyebrows at her in that maddening way she just might—

"What is it?" He had the nerve to look surprised, and that made Kitty even angrier.

"Why did you take over the conversation like that?" she demanded. "And tell that sob story about me—"

Laurence frowned. "I was introducing you and your charity—"

*"Foundation,"* she stressed. "And I thought the point of this was that I'd talk for *myself*."

"What's the difference? We're here as a couple."

Kitty wondered if flames were shooting out of her head—her face certainly felt hot enough. She counted backwards from ten in her head before speaking. "*I* talk about my business. Not you. And you definitely don't get to talk about my past, or how I grew up. Not now, not ever!"

"Kitty—"

"You know how the Senator is off-limits as a topic of conversation? My past is off-limits to you," she said firmly.

She was trying to sound calm, but she knew her frustration was leaching into her voice.

"Kitty, I didn't tell them anything," Laurence argued back.

Although he seemed fascinated by her anger as her chest heaved, her body hummed with awareness. In one irrational moment she wondered if he would reach out, grasp her by the wrists, pull her flush against his body, test her to the breaking point—

She took a full step back. "Just watch yourself," she hissed, and stalked away from him.

The defiant gesture was just a little too much

for the delicate sandals Cordelia had forced on her, and she felt her ankle turn. She stumbled, but Laurence was there in a flash, his hands at her waist.

"These things will be the death of you," he said gently, very close to her ear.

"Let me *go*," she said, giving him a push for good measure. She was steady on her feet—and, thank God, there was no throbbing. She tried to take a step and almost lost her footing again. The buckle had either loosened or broken. She swore.

"Very ladylike," Laurence said, and before she could stop him he was on one knee in front of her, those big hands cradling her ankle. "Let me see, honey."

His voice was neutral, but his hands were anything but. His thumbs pressed down, and she inhaled sharply.

"Hurts?"

"No." A lightning-hot frisson went through her at the caress on her skin. His grip was firm without being constricting; his fingers were warm. Strong. She gulped. "I'm *fine*."

Laurence began to rotate her foot, saying nothing, and Kitty felt warmer by the second. It was a warmth that had little to do with the late-afternoon sun beating down on their heads.

Several feet ahead of them, Giles and Doris turned.

"Proposing already, Laurence?" Doris called.

Laurence laughed out loud and mimed removing a ring from his pocket, then turned his attention back to Kitty's ankle. "Nosy old bag," he muttered.

"I really am all right..." How could her voice go from furious to breathy in only a few seconds?

"It's not broken. The strap just slipped out from the buckle," Laurence said, and began doing up the thin strap with more dexterity than she would have thought in a man of that size.

He was also maddeningly slow, and occasionally his fingertips skimmed her skin in a way that left her insides quivering. She'd never thought of the foot as a particularly erogenous zone, but now she could sense the dampness forming between her thighs.

She bit back a groan, as much from frustration as from arousal. *I'm not going to be able to do this.* She concentrated on breathing instead, on slowing the rapid beating of her heart and not giving any sign that she felt what she did.

When he'd finished Laurence stood. As it had been the night at the Park Hotel his finery was virtually undisturbed except for his pocket square, which was doing its best to escape. The Muellers were no longer in sight, and when his eyes skimmed her face they did so as Laurence Stone, not as the manipulative businessman telling whatever story he had to in order to close a deal.

"I'm sorry," he said simply, and offered her his arm.

Kitty felt rather light-headed, both from their argument and from what had happened afterwards. She licked her lips. "It's fine."

Perhaps to confirm that this was indeed a truce, she reached up to adjust the errant square of pale fabric.

When he took a startled step back she even managed a smile. "I'm not going to hit you."

"A man can't be too careful."

Kitty went about her work and put it back as quickly as she could. It felt oddly intimate, doing this for him.

"Hey…"

She looked up.

"I'm on your side, Kitty."

*And I don't want to fight with you…not really.*

Laurence Stone was by far the most confusing man she'd ever interacted with. Most of the time she wanted to kill him, other times his unrelenting dryness made her laugh against her will, and at yet other times she wanted him to press her hard against the nearest surface, pin her down, kiss her until she couldn't breathe.

The possibility of feeling real affection for this man at some point was there, and it was terrifying. Unexpected.

She pressed her lips together and stepped back, then took Laurence's offered arm in silence.

By the time the races began Kitty had three new sponsors and found her confidence growing with each conversation. Laurence was much more amiable—introducing her to guests one by one and then letting her steer the conversation.

They sat side by side for the duration of the race, silent in the face of the chattering crowd and thundering hooves, and when they were shielded by the chatter and the cheers of their companions, he turned to her and smiled.

"Having fun?"

Kitty took a breath. She was glad they'd made up, in some odd way. Laurence wasn't *terrible* company when he was being...tolerable. Not nice, she told herself. She'd never call him *nice*— not with that perpetual smirk.

"I was more nervous than I thought I'd be,"

she admitted. "I've pitched before, but…" She trailed off. "It's different, being here as someone's girlfriend. Not crashing."

He nodded. "You did all right."

*All right?* Kitty's eyes narrowed. "High praise, coming from a—"

"You did *fine*," Laurence said laconically. "Two-minute list of bullet points…almost verbatim from that heinous website."

Kitty stared at him, half considering turning her glass of champagne into his lap. Had she really thought only moments ago that they might find some common ground? "This isn't my first time doing this, you know, and the fact that they committed to a donation—"

"Meant that they would do anything to get you to stop talking." Laurence smiled, an unexpected flash of white in his face. When Kitty sputtered, he shook his head. "I do this for a living. I'm not trying to undermine you every time I make a criticism."

*Yes, you are.*

Otherwise he wouldn't take so much pleasure in it.

However, curiosity won out. "How would you do it differently? I was concise and friendly.

Elevator pitch. There shouldn't be anything more or I'd be dominating the conversation."

"And why shouldn't you?" Laurence half turned to smile at her again.

He'd donned a straw boater, tipped forward over his eyes; on him the ridiculous hat looked good, and she suspected he knew it.

"We're stuck in this tacky booth, dressed like refugees from *The Great Gatsby*, and we're both after fat wads of cash. It's all about acting, Kitty. Storytelling is a vital part of selling. I don't talk about myself, either, but I make up plenty. Just take enough of the truth to fit the situation and have fun with it."

Kitty frowned.

"Think of it this way…" he said, and shifted so he was a bit closer to her.

She could see Doris Mueller just outside the line of vision, looking at them and mouthing *How sweet*, nudging her husband. She could not protest when he drew her close.

"You've already fascinated them," he said simply. "You're beautiful, and intelligent, and compassionate, and kindness radiates from every word you say."

Each word lit a little spark in Kitty, so when he'd finished she felt as if a fire had been kindled low in her chest. It was a warmth that had little to do with desire and everything to do with— Well… She'd spent years working hard with barely anyone's notice. She'd told herself long ago that she didn't even care to have it, but—

"Are you sure that's not a line?" she said gruffly.

Laurence smiled thinly, then spoke again, this time into her ear. "Think on this…" he said, and there was the barest warmth of his lips against her ear canal.

Kitty could not think at all—not with him so close. He smelled like rum and spice, a living embodiment of everything rich and refined…and his hand was fitted into the curve of her waist as if it belonged there. She could feel her body relaxing into his as if the heat radiating from his frame was melting the ice she'd been encased in all this while. It was absolutely surreal.

Below them she could see the horses on the track, their gleaming sides heaving with exertion. Laurence was still talking, low and gentle. She tilted her head so that his nose and mouth fit perfectly into the crook of her neck and shivered as he drew her closer. Closed her eyes.

"The story of us, for example," he began.

"There is no 'us,'" she murmured.

"Quiet, you'll ruin it." He laughed softly.

Kitty wanted to pull away as badly as she wanted to stay, and Laurence's grip tightened on her as if he knew it.

"There's a moment of danger," Laurence was saying now, against her skin. "A flash…completely unexpected. There's a man, and a woman, and she's young and vivid, with perfect skin—" here, Laurence nipped at the edge of her jaw, making her jump a little before he soothed it with the softest of kisses "—and eyes that could hypnotize a man."

*Oh.* Kitty's cheeks warmed. But Laurence held her fast, still talking softly. All that mattered was the feel of him, how close he was, how *right* it felt.

Laurence was incorrigible, but—yes… There were those flashes of kindness sometimes, and amusement, and other things that had her studying his face when she knew he wasn't looking.

He was still talking. About *them*.

"They're still covered in dirt, see, and gravel… and they're trembling because they just escaped death. But there's a spark, and he's holding her like she's the most fragile thing he's ever touched, because at that moment she is. And the world, for that moment, is reduced only to them…lying on that bit of dirty concrete while the city races past."

His lips were hovering over hers now, and he lifted his brows. And Kitty felt a sigh emit from her lips *just* as they met. This was not mocking, or drunk, or possessive. It was gentle, almost loving, and that part of her she'd trained never to need affection roared to life.

When they parted Kitty blinked hard, speechless and trembling like a leaf...or a virgin...or at the very least someone who wasn't practically seated in the lap of the most inappropriate man in all of Manhattan.

"I think you're full of crap," she managed, licking her lips and drawing herself up.

His laughter rang in the small space, and to her discomfort it was just as warming as his kiss had been.

"I told you what I do, Kitty. It's precisely that— I sell stories. The beauty isn't in what *is*—it's in what *could be*, if we lived in an ideal world and things like that happened. It's not lying. It's giving a consumer a story they want to hear. Making them feel good about themselves. Creating a personal connection. And if they've all watched fate bring us together, watched us fall in *love*—"

his mouth bent a little at the word "—they'll follow the story as long as it lasts."

*As long as it lasts.*

Kitty shifted, feeling curiously bereft. With every moment that passed she felt all the more foolish for her reaction. Whatever Laurence made her feel, it wasn't real, and she would do best to remember that.

"You're a fraud," she said crossly, pushing back against him, though with much less conviction than she wanted.

He laughed again, and when he slid his arms round her she didn't protest. In fact, she let her body relax against his.

She could not deny that whatever she thought of Laurence, this felt—nice.

"I'm a very rich fraud. And you'll be one too, if you play along."

# CHAPTER NINE

AFTER THEIR DAY at the races, Laurence and Kitty fell into an easy rhythm—one that was punctuated by what Laurence called "small, smart affairs." There was a trip to see a jazz pianist, a night at a Broadway show, one lunch, two dinners, all with current and potential clients, or with members of New York's corporate society.

Kitty was growing dangerously used to being ferried about in a Mercedes in clothes that could have paid her rent for months, and she repeated her goal—*the success of her foundation*—as a mantra to herself every time she went out with Laurence for any reason. She'd received more donations in that couple of weeks than she had the entire previous year, and her little roster of clients was growing.

One morning Cordelia called her, bright and early.

"There's an opportunity for you to speak about

One Step Ahead for the morning news," she said briskly. "Laurence asked me if you'd be interested."

*Interested?* She'd have to be mad not to be. "Yes, I'm interested."

"Very well. I'll send you the details."

A spot on a nationally broadcast TV program! Kitty went into a mix of elation and sheer terror.

A day later an agent from the network contacted her. She was to have a seven-minute spot with Laurence, to talk about philanthropy and her work in the city.

When she hung up Kitty dug into her files, read notes from other presentations she'd done in the past. Nothing seemed right for television, or for the easy-breezy format of the show. It usually featured summer cocktails, juggling, and dog-grooming as regular topics.

Laurence was right. Her usual speech was *boring*. It was as boring as drying concrete. It read like a brochure that you might find in the back pocket of a taxicab and read because you were running late and your mobile was flat.

Defeated, she rang Laurence.

He picked up almost immediately. "Is that the love of my—?"

"I'll never forgive you if you aren't serious about this."

"What's the matter, Kitty?" She could hear mild curiosity in his voice.

"Cordelia called me and told me about speaking on—"

"Oh, the news segment." He sounded as if he were prepared to be very pleased with himself.

"My presentation isn't right," she admitted. "And I have no idea why."

"Are you nervous?"

"The fact that I'm calling you voluntarily should tell you plenty."

"Ah."

He was silent so long she spoke again. "Laurence?"

He made a noise deep in his throat, and she fought the flush creeping up her neck. Laurence had been very good at keeping his hands to himself since their day at the races, and Kitty had been appalled at each meeting to find herself almost disappointed. Her brain recoiled at the idea of his hands on her, but her body missed it. Now even just the sound of his voice—

She forced herself to attention.

"When I make a presentation," he said calmly,

"I think first about what the audience needs to know—not about nervousness."

"You get nervous?"

"Never—because that method works." For once there was no hint of mockery in his tone. "The success of my business lies on my ability to make people care about what I'm saying. Think about your audience, Kitty. Think about what they don't know, what they need to know—and the fact that you're the expert on it, not them."

Kitty found herself nodding on the other end of the line. She knew all this, of course, but it was soothing, hearing it from Laurence's mouth. "Okay."

"And…" He paused. Then, "Don't be afraid to talk a little about yourself. Not gratuitously, but just so that people know you believe in them and that's why you're helping them. Empathy."

There was another long silence. Laurence apparently had nothing more to say, but Kitty found herself wanting to prolong the conversation, for some reason. "Are you busy?"

"I'm in a meeting with Desmond and a stakeholder."

"There are *people* there?" Kitty squeaked.

"You know I put you first, sweetheart."

Laurence chuckled softly, sending ripples of

want through her body. She was beginning to associate this involuntary quiver with the sound of Laurence's voice when it dropped to that intimate timbre, and she despaired over it. He could be infuriating, but he also could be—

"I have to go," she said, her face flaming, and she ended the call.

On the day of the interview Laurence took Kitty to the studio at four, when many people were beginning to head home. They were to pre-record their segment and it would air the next day. She'd looked more relieved than he'd ever seen her when he'd told her about the pre-recording.

"I was nervous about going live," she admitted now, and he shrugged.

"I don't want to be broadcast live either," he said.

"Why? Because you're with me?" Kitty snapped, offended.

God, the woman could get her back up at a moment's notice! He felt as if he were constantly trying to defend his motives.

"You're very self-centered, Kitty. This is my first in-person interview in over a year. I hate them, but Desmond pushed for it. Not everything I do is about you."

Kitty looked surprised at his honesty, and perhaps a little chastised, but she had no time to reply. They were immediately shown to a trailer, where Kitty was made up with pots and sticks of makeup of varying hues, then attacked with a powder puff the size of her head.

When the makeup artist who'd been assaulting her cheeks stopped, Kitty sneezed.

"You're perfect," the woman gushed, then took her basket and scurried out of the trailer they'd been assigned, eager to move on to the next guest.

Kitty wrinkled her nose, clearly trying not to sneeze again. She was wearing far more makeup than he'd ever seen on her—even at the party where they'd reconnected. He didn't like it. It made her skin look waxy and grayish, and exaggerated her eyes and lips almost to caricature.

She touched her face as if she'd read his mind. "It's not my color. I know I look like a cadaver."

He exhaled with a short laugh.

"I'm worried about talking about—about us on live television…" Her brows knitted together; she looked troubled. "I don't like lying. You joke about the food thing, but this is different. And if your parents ever found out—"

Laurence barely kept the white-hot anger that

sparked in him at the mention of the two of them from crossing his face. "Even if I married you atop the Empire State Building they'd never say a word," he said sharply. "They are no longer in my life and I've taken legal action to make sure it stays that way!"

Kitty's brown eyes were as round as basketballs. "What happened?"

Laurence swore inwardly. Not many people knew about his break with his parents, and hearing Kitty ask about it had caught him quite off guard.

"Were you *listening* when I spoke about the tax fraud before, Kitty? My father is a manipulative bastard, and my mother is a spineless trophy wife," he said, allowing all the bitterness he felt to drip from every word. Instead of ducking his head, he forced himself to look directly at her. "You should know that better than anyone, Kitty. Did you *really* think you were anything but a ploy for his campaign?"

She swallowed hard.

"Think about it," he snapped. "You know how readily they discarded you. That's what they did, Kitty, when you were no longer useful."

He was saying too much...getting too emotional. If Kitty chose to prolong the conversation, to dig—

*Shut up, Laurence!*

He turned away from her to fiddle with his cuff. When he'd composed himself and looked back at her, Kitty had already arranged her features into neutrality.

"I'm very sorry," she said softly, as if she'd just realized something.

"It's fine." He was already regretting his outburst, but he would not allude to it now. "And you'll be fine out there. The general viewing public are idiots, mostly."

"It's more likely that people will be scared of me." She pointed to her face.

Laurence's mouth twitched. "My mother always took her own makeup to shoots," he said.

And with those words it was as if he were transported back to his childhood, watching his mother mutter about how makeup artists *"never got it right"* while handing over foundation custom-blended for the deep tints of her smooth skin. Memory was like that: it eased through the anger he felt when he thought about her from time to time, as subtle as smoke through cracks in a wall.

*"Enhance, don't smother,"* she'd command. *"A light hand. My skin doesn't need help to glow."*

Kitty's didn't need help either. Even in the harsh fluorescent light of the trailer, even beneath that horrible makeup job, she was radiant.

Abruptly Laurence eased out of the high-backed makeup chair and crossed over to Kitty, who leaned back.

"What?"

"Have you got your own makeup with you?" he asked.

"Some—"

"You're right. It's dreadful," he said, letting amusement leak into his voice. "Hold still and lift your chin—I'll help you get it off. You might stain your dress."

As he talked he ripped open the pack of wet wipes on the vanity in front of them.

"She worked so hard at it," Kitty said, wavering.

"Up to you, but you look like you're on the set of *Dynasty*." He paused. "Or a clown."

That was enough for Kitty. She huffed as she leaned back, but allowed Laurence to clean her face with gentle swipes at her cheeks, lips, lids. The makeup came off easily, and her body, so close to his, was as tense as it was warm.

"Should I wonder why you're so well accus-

tomed with women's makeup and *Dynasty*?"
Kitty said after a moment, barely moving her lips.

He laughed without smiling. "Supermodel
mother with a soap opera addiction." The woman
also enjoyed shopping, and social activities, and
always looked vaguely exhausted…as if the
weight of wealth was far too much for her.

"Oh. That's right…"

"I traveled with her until my father decided he
wanted to run for public office. Then she didn't
have time for me anymore." He felt an odd pang
as he said it. He'd signed his mother off as well
as his father—complicity was the same as guilt
in his head—but he did miss her at times.

Kitty opened her eyes, and Laurence felt an
odd charge.

"Thank you, Laurence," she said, after a moment.

"For what?"

His name on her lips had sounded oddly intimate in this space, with him cleaning her skin.
He reached for a small hand towel and turned
on the tap in the sink to the right of the vanity.
The water that came out was clear and hot. He
soaked the towel, wrung it out.

"Last spa treatment," he said, and reached out
to press the warm washcloth to her cheeks.

A little exhalation of pleasure burst from that full mouth and he felt his body respond. He had not allowed himself to think about how readily his blood surged in response to her closeness. It would not be right.

"That feels like heaven," she murmured, and closed her eyes again, surrendering completely to the warm compress soothing her skin.

Laurence cleared his throat and spoke to cover the silence. "You'll do great."

Her skin had taken on a rosy tinge beneath the smooth chestnut, both from the heat and their close proximity. When he set the towel down, she sighed.

"Thank you," she said again.

"Right."

She was close enough to kiss, and her lashes, long and lush, cast half-moon shadows on her cheeks. She wouldn't look at him, but he wanted her to. Desperately.

"Kitty..." he murmured, and touched her chin.

When she opened her eyes his stomach plummeted to his knees. For the first time since they'd reconnected she resembled the girl he remembered.

Her eyes were bright, and she swallowed hard before she spoke. "I'm scared," she admitted.

It was barely a whisper, but it still felt loud. "Lying? On live television?"

Laurence forced himself to laugh. He did not feel very much like laughing—not at all—but if Kitty continued down this path the interview would be a disaster, and he could not afford that.

It worked as he'd intended. Kitty's eyes narrowed, and she sat up. *Good.* Better she be angry than a moralizing train wreck.

"Why on earth are you laughing?" she asked.

He lifted his fingers to touch the base of her chin with careful fingers. "Because you're being absurd. Remember, Kitty. You're doing this to skim money from the wallets of people who don't give until they feel absolutely splendid about themselves. For most of them it's a drop in the bucket and a huge tax write-off. Kitty…?"

The turmoil in those lovely eyes and the softness of her lips and skin were altogether too tempting. He moved closer, allowed his lips to brush the sensual curve that was the corner of her mouth.

*Just one kiss.*

Kitty felt a wave of despair. This wasn't going right at all. She felt dizzy now—dizzy from his closeness, and the scent of him, and the fact that, yes, they were probably going to kiss again, and she wouldn't be able to blame him for it this time.

Her body was throbbing as hard as her heart was beating, and Laurence— Well… He made her so angry—the angriest she'd ever been since his father had dealt with her, years ago—but he also had a way of looking at her that made her want to cover her face and weep.

It was as if he saw straight through the facade to the girl inside, who still shrank when she thought of how she'd been abandoned by the Stones. He'd been ruthless, almost cruel, but he'd always been there so far, and that was something.

Kitty's head tilted back, as if in response to an unspoken question, and when the length of his body finally pressed against hers her body coiled with tension, but also with relief. Whatever the ramifications were, she'd never wanted anyone so badly in her life.

"You're going to do wonderfully. You are beautiful, and brilliant, and I'm honored to have you work with me," Laurence said quietly, his lips very close to hers. "Fake or not, that is real."

His hands lifted to grip her hips, tugging her flush against him. His lids were hanging so low she could not see his eyes, and that for some reason bothered her more than anything else. She gave in to an impulse, reached out and cupped the sides of his face with her hands. Her next breath came out as a sigh.

"Laurence…" she whispered.

This was a terrible idea, a ghastly idea, and in more ways than one. But here, so close to him, it all seemed so elemental. She was a woman, with wetness now pooling between her thighs. He was a man, a very attractive one, and if the hardness pressing against her abdomen was any indication he was much in the same situation. And if they didn't somehow clear the air…somehow get rid of the attraction that had dogged them both since she'd seen him at that party almost a lifetime ago—

She dropped her fingers down to the wall of his chest, sliding them over his abdomen. What she found hinted deliciously at muscle as finely carved as rock, but when her fingers dropped lower his hand flashed out, stilling her exploration.

"No," he said.

She felt a wave of mortification that only lasted a second, because he was pressing her against the back of her chair and kissing her as if he'd no other intent that afternoon. Unlike the kiss in his office, which had been slow and a little tentative, this was rougher, harder—as if he were trying to make a point or scare her off.

Well, she had her own point to make, and her frustrations vented themselves in this heated clash of lips and skin.

When they finally surfaced for air, she let out a ragged gasp and lifted her chin. For the first time ever since this whole miserable situation had begun she felt as if she had the upper hand—and it was all because of his dilated pupils, the heated look on his face. No one had ever looked at her like that, and her body thrummed with awareness.

"I think you like this," she managed, emulating the mocking tone he always used with her.

His mouth turned down at one corner and his reply was to apply his lips to her ear, let them travel to the side of her neck.

Kitty bit the inside of her cheek—hard. *Bastard.* He knew it was a sensitive spot for her. She realized that even at this early stage he was so in tune to her body that any lovemaking between them would be explosive.

"So sweet…" he whispered against her skin.

The warning bells pealing in her head faded. In this moment, she was completely and utterly lost.

# CHAPTER TEN

IF KITTY DIDN'T stop squirming like that, Laurence thought, struggling to keep his breaths even and deep, this would be over before it began.

Not that he should have begun anything. He was aware of that—more aware than he'd ever been of anything. This…thing, whatever it was, had been hanging between them since the weekend they'd met, and it had to come to a head one way or another.

He allowed himself the pleasure of touching her breasts for a moment, cupping their full weight in his hands, marveling at how the softness overflowed. Her nipples hardened at his touch, even through layers of silk and lace—but they were not his target for now.

Thank God she was wearing a skirt…

His fingers dropped to her hips, gathering a handful of soft, diaphanous fabric and pushing it up her legs, revealing inch after inch of glowing rich skin.

But even in Laurence's most out-of-control moments his pragmatism reared its head, and today was no exception. If he was going to do this here, with Kitty Asare of all people, it had to be about fleeting pleasure and nothing else. He could not risk a connection. In his mind, if not in reality, this had to be as banal as he could make it. Kitty Asare was not an option for anything more.

It wasn't just that he might break her heart—he realized he'd already done that, ten years ago. It was that he couldn't risk his own. Not with someone so absolutely unsuitable.

Kitty's eyes were hazy and soft…beckoning, almost. He kissed her lightly, slid his hands up the inside of her thighs. The skin there was the softest he'd touched in a very long time, warm, quivering beneath his palms. He stroked her inner thighs gently, almost absent-mindedly, his eyes still glued to her face.

It was as variable as the sky, and as lovely. In the few moments he'd been looking he'd registered wonder, self-consciousness, irritation and—yes—arousal. Plenty of it. His own body was surging to answer hers, but for a moment—just a moment—he wanted to look at her. He wanted to give her pleasure.

She shifted. "Well?" she gritted out, breaking into his thoughts. And he laughed.

"Greedy," he said gently, and rested his forehead against hers. "This is disastrous," he added under his breath, surprising himself as the words came out.

Kitty laughed raggedly. "No kidding."

What *was* this, then? An attempt at self-indulgence for both of them?

He did not ask. Instead he cupped her through the thin layer of lace-covered silk that was his last barrier to the heat that was warming his palm. Her head tipped back. He began to trace over the feathery pattern on the lace slowly, thumbing it aside when he saw her bite her lip, then tugging it down to one ankle, impatiently. There was a downy softness first, and then, where he parted her, a silken wetness that made his own heart beat faster, the blood throb between his legs to the point of pain.

"Spread your thighs a little more…" he husked out. "There… That's good…"

Now there was a sweet, heady musk that made him ache to taste her, though there wasn't time. Damn it, there wasn't time, even though his mouth watered for her. The little bud of arousal between her folds was swollen, protruding

through the soft pinkness that hid it, and so slick
he actually groaned, then bent his head anyway.

*Just one taste.*

Kitty did cry out then, in pleasured shock, and
jerked forward against his mouth. His laugh was
muffled between her legs as he lapped at her
sweetness, sucked gently. She'd been ready, and
for much longer than they'd been in this room.
Her whole body was tensed, coiled, ready to
snap. He wanted her to break at that moment, to
come undone in his arms.

He only allowed himself a moment, then resur-
faced reluctantly. They had to finish this much
faster than he wanted. Her small hands dropped
down to where he strained against his trousers
and he reached out and stopped her.

*"No,"* he gritted out. Her touching him would
mean she was taking control of the situation, and
that would not do. He palmed her thighs, eased
them open again.

She looked both agitated and frustrated, but
her face contorted in shock and pleasure as he
slipped a finger inside her. He felt her inner walls
clamp down instantly. She cried out and he let
her pitch forward, pressing her face into his neck.
He would have preferred her head to stay back,
so he could see her face, but she shook her head.

"That's it…ride it out," he said gently.

And then Kitty was moving her hips in determined circles, her lips warm and damp on his neck, mouthing words he'd never get to hear. It didn't take long, and yet he'd lost all sense of time when she cried out, spending herself on his fingertips.

They were both reduced to gasps for air and accelerated heartbeats and warm damp skin for several seconds, and then they began to emerge, separating back into their own bodies.

Kitty had gone limp in his arms. He withdrew his hand from beneath her skirt, clearing his throat. She was still hiding her face. He did not speak, but he nosed her cheek, her neck.

"For a fake girlfriend, I think you can be pretty convincing," he rasped after a moment.

He knew it was awful, but he had to do something about the throbbing between his legs, and breaking the mood would help.

"Oh—you!"

Kitty's voice still did not sound quite normal, but she did swat at him, scrambling for the flimsy scrap of lace still hanging off one ankle.

She opened her mouth to speak again, but exactly at that moment there was a knock at the trailer door.

"We'll need you out in fifteen," a man's voice called.

Kitty began to frantically rearrange her dress. When Laurence tried to help her she batted his hands away furiously.

"You've done enough!" she whispered.

"He said fifteen minutes, Kitty, not fifteen seconds."

She closed her eyes again. "You're not normal," she murmured.

"Yes," he agreed. "That being said, you need to re-do your makeup, and I—"

He gestured down to where he still strained against his trousers. They'd never felt so tight before, and he was using every trick he'd learned since puberty to take his mind off how much he wanted to take care of it, to bury himself deep inside her.

"This will take some time to go."

"Oh." She looked faintly embarrassed, then hunched her shoulders and reached for her handbag. She fumbled out a lipstick, a compact, and numerous little jars that he couldn't identify. "I won't take long."

He could have just stood there, with the massive erection that showed no inclination to wane, but he took pity on her instead, and turned. "I've got a couple of emails to answer," he said.

"Woman of the hour," Laurence greeted her sarcastically when the interview was over and Kitty had emerged from the trailer dressed in her street clothes.

He took in her torn jeans and black tank top with the usual hitch of his brow, but Kitty couldn't care less. She could have left on the fine designer dress, but after that afternoon she wanted nothing more than to shed the illusion, get back to being Kitty Asare.

"How did you find it, sweetheart?"

"Don't call me that." She'd intended to be curt, but her voice came out as something else entirely: soft as silk. Affectionate. Almost yielding...as if this was part of their own special banter. "There's no one around to hear, is there?"

"There's always someone around, Kitty." He reached out, closing a big hand round the handle of her garment bag, and she was startled enough to let him take it. "I meant it when I said that you did well. I was thoroughly impressed."

Kitty felt her cheeks warm despite herself. She'd taken his advice while in front of the camera, spoken slowly and carefully, concentrated on nothing but the memory of every young person she'd been able to help, and Laurence—in rare form—had deferred to her on almost every question. Their interviewer, a journalist of high repute, had seemed genuinely interested, and had followed up with an email a bare half-hour later, asking for Kitty's details. Listeners, she said, were already clamoring to donate.

"You did, too," she said after a beat.

Laurence lifted his shoulders, as if it was of little importance, then raised his phone to look at it. "I've gotten messages from people who haven't spoken to me since college, asking about you."

Kitty pressed her hands to her cheeks. "Surely you dating someone can't be that unusual?"

He shrugged. He looked as if he had something else to say, but his next words were a question. "Dinner?"

Kitty started. "Excuse me?"

"Dinner. With me." His voice was staccato, clipped. "Pretty natural thing for a couple to do after a day out, no?"

"I—I guess so."

Her heart gave an odd little jump. Was this part of the agreement? After-hours dates? He was looking at her so intensely. Especially after what had happened in the trailer. Heat engulfed her as she remembered the feel of his lips on her neck, her thighs…

"Great. We'll take the car." Laurence paused, looked at his ever-present smartphone. "I'm sure that Cordelia will want to arrange for us to be photographed, so you might want to change back into your dress."

*Oh.* So this *was* a work thing, then. Kitty pushed aside a feeling of disappointment.

"No," she said rebelliously, and Laurence looked up. "I'm satisfied with my outfit."

"Suit yourself."

"*Ghanaian* food?" Kitty exclaimed as soon as they walked into the restaurant.

Laurence's face creased into a smile—one that did reach his eyes. He looked pleased at her surprise, genuinely pleased.

"Do you like it? It was a gamble," he replied, laughing as Kitty stared wide-eyed at a menu.

"I didn't know there was anything like this in Hell's Kitchen!"

"The owner's an old friend of my mother's." His lips tipped up. "I know you've been in the States since you were small, so I didn't know if you'd like the food, but…" He lifted his shoulders. "Americans eat here, too. It's good either way."

The African fusion restaurant had no visible sign, no prices on the menu, and was so dark inside that candlelight danced off the planes of Laurence's face with all the drama of a black and white film. It smelled of frying meat, curry, smoke, and tallow, and still managed to be ridiculously romantic.

"It feels like a private club," Kitty said excitedly as they took their seats.

She'd had African food in New York before, of course, but nowhere this chic or trendy. The menu offered Moroccan, Nigerian and Ghanaian dishes, and the owner—a tall, thin man in a funky interpretation of traditional dress—came to pour ruby wine from an impressively dusty bottle.

"*Mema wo adwo*, sir," he said, and flashed Kitty a smile after the greeting. "You brought a beautiful lady, I see. Finally."

"I usually eat with Desmond, and they're all sick of him," Laurence explained dryly, and the man chuckled.

"Pleased to meet you, ma'am. Please relax. I will bring you some of everything."

The other diners were dressed in varying levels

of casual and formal, and entirely wrapped up in their own conversations. If anyone was going to take photographs, Kitty had no idea how they'd do it discreetly.

Their food arrived: savory, peppery *jollof* rice, delicately flavored with chicken and thyme, smoky broiled fish on a bed of sweet onions and peppers, *kontomire* stew, rich with tomatoes and oil, with fork-tender coco-yam to absorb the delicious liquid.

Kitty fell on the meal with enthusiasm. It was impossible to recreate masterpieces like this in the shared kitchen of her apartment.

Laurence was a little more restrained, but he was amused. "You look as if you want to climb on the platter and roll around," he said, dryly, piling her plate again.

Kitty laughed and soaked up the last of her stew with a bit of yam. "I just might."

Laurence was looking at her as if she were a puzzle he was keen to solve, and if he had any sarcasm, he kept it to himself.

"I enjoyed today," he said after a moment.

Kitty met his eyes, and then she blushed. There was heat there, reminiscent of when he'd had her pinned in the trailer, a hand up her skirt. Now his gaze seemed to penetrate her very soul.

Perhaps it was the wine, or perhaps it was the haze that her earlier encounter with Laurence had left, lulling her brain into a post-coital fuzz of sorts. The afternoon had been a complete Cinderella moment—except the Prince was using her, and he'd teased her to orgasm with his fingers in a public place.

*None of it is real.*

Kitty bit her lip and shifted, feeling that now-familiar pull between her legs. Laurence Stone was proving himself rather quickly to be an enigma, and one she had no business trying to figure out.

"Kitty."

"Mmm…?"

"Tell me," Laurence said, almost too quiet to be heard even in that intimate space. "What it was like for you after you left."

The serenity of the moment was shattered. Kitty blinked. "Why?"

"Just tell me."

"It was a long time ago, Laurence—"

He shook his head and leaned forward. In the weak light of the restaurant his eyes were two burning coals deep in his face. "I'd like to know. Please," he added, and waited.

Kitty spoke. She didn't know what compelled

her to speak, but she did. "I went back into care," she said, and the words came out curiously flat.

There was no way—not even if she had the most eloquent vocabulary and all the time in the world—she could convey in a few short moments the pain of rejection that had plagued her that year.

"I lost my place at prep school." It still hurt, after all these years. "Went to public school. I was eyeing NYU, but that was out of the question. I got into City College."

"Where did you live?"

Her lips tightened. *Group houses. Shelters.* Places she'd never admit to this lofty, arrogant businessman who wanted to know far too much. She claimed that her living arrangements now were to save money, but if Kitty looked deep down inside herself she knew it was because she was terrified to look for anything more permanent. It was foolish, but she almost felt as if settling down, finding happiness, would tempt fate into snatching it from her.

"There are places," she said, "for people who need help."

"Shelters?"

"We call them group homes. They're nice," she added, staring him down, daring him to rebuff the lie. He didn't. "After that I bunked with my caseworker for a month, and then I moved on campus. Got my degree and—" She shrugged. "That was it."

A muscle worked in his cheek. "Was it very difficult?"

How the hell was she supposed to answer that question? She'd never starved, though she'd lived on the worst possible food, and she'd never slept outside, though she'd come close some nights, when there had been a shortage of beds in her group house, or other residents had made her feel unsafe.

Still, those things paled in comparison to her emotional state. She'd fallen into a depression so deep that some days getting out of bed and brushing her teeth was too hard. She'd been lonely, and confused, and she had ached, continually, with the feeling of losing something she wasn't even sure had been hers to lose.

"Kitty?"

She swallowed. "I—I felt *rejected*, Laurence. Anyone would."

He was silent for such a long time that Kitty finally dared to peek at his face. Her insides were churning, as if being twisted by a hand. Laurence's face looked dark and forbidding. He also

looked faintly sick and, despite herself, something in her cried out for him in a way that had
little to do with sex. It was something more to
do with shared experiences, shared trauma—
and perhaps she was recognizing the pain that
flitted across his face because she too had worn
the same expression once or twice.

"We should go," was all he said, and he placed
his fork down. Neither had eaten much after Kitty's monologue; the air was too thick with things
unsaid.

She nodded, stared at her plate until he'd paid,
and then walked out with him. She did not resist
when he took her hand in his or stood close to
her as they waited for his car to muscle its way
to the curb.

"Mason will take you home," he said, looking
down at her.

That unnerving softness was still in his eyes.
It was as if he were looking at her, really looking
at her, for the first time, and it was terrifying.

"Thank you for dinner." She forced a smile.
"Not bad for a fake boyfriend."

"Right…" He cleared his throat.

"It's too bad we won't be able to—"

Kitty was unable to finish the casual sentence
she was attempting for Laurence had stepped

forward, closed the distance between them. His big hands closed over her arms. Firmly. Gently.

"Is it all right?" he asked after a beat.

Dumbly, Kitty nodded.

Laurence kissed her softly. She'd thought she'd experienced the full range of his kisses, but this one was entirely different; it sparked warmth without igniting a fire and it was disconcertingly gentle. He explored her mouth leisurely, retreating and coming back, as if he were trying to tell her something he had no words for.

When he pulled back, she was surprised. She wasn't breathless this time. In fact, she breathed the deepest she had in ages and the air seemed clearer. Sweeter.

"Why?" she whispered.

There was an oddly cool stickiness between her thighs, where his fingers and his mouth had teased her sex hours earlier. She wanted to shower, let the water beat down on her and wash the feeling of him away. Not because it had been bad—it had been the opposite. But she could not afford to think of it as anything more than—

"I don't know," he said, and she saw his throat constrict.

## CHAPTER ELEVEN

WHEN KITTY OPENED the door of her apartment the next day to collect the newspaper she smelled the flowers before she saw them. They were excessively bright, tropical and in bloom, sitting on her front step in a delicate Tiffany-style vase of stained glass, brightening the dirty hallway with vivid bursts of crimson and yellow and blue. The colors were like none she'd ever seen in nature, and she reached out and touched a petal tentatively before picking up the heavy cream card peeking out from beneath the vase's brim.

The card was written in a thick, heavy hand. She guessed it was from Laurence before she even saw what it said.

*Forgive me for my deplorable behavior.*
*You were remarkable.*

Kitty held the card close to her chest for a moment, then dropped it as if it were red-hot. She could not afford such sentiment—not with

Laurence Stone, despite whatever odd moments they'd shared.

She chewed her lip, then focused on getting dressed. Tonight was the *pièce de resistance*—an intimate dinner, hosted out on Long Island for several of his clients, introducing the Muellers to the "family."

"It's the Long Island house," Laurence had told her a week before their interview. "You would have stayed there while you were with…them."

"I did," Kitty said through dry lips.

*The Stone estate.* Her heart thudded in her chest.

"My grandfather left it to me. He died a few years back. I'll never live there, but I do use it for entertaining. My place isn't suitable for dining. If it isn't all right with you, though—"

"Why wouldn't it be all right with me?" Kitty spoke rapidly, cutting in to disabuse him of that notion. "Are the Muellers signing?"

"They're close."

"And what's wrong with a hotel?"

"The Muellers enjoy personal attention. Home-cooked meals. *Eccentricity*," Laurence said, as if he could not quite believe that anyone would want to socialize that way. "We did our research.

One of the reasons they left their last client was that he didn't treat them like *family*."

Kitty felt a wild desire to laugh. Family? Her and Laurence? With their background? There couldn't be two people who knew less about it.

Laurence's eyes flickered over her face quickly, and he smiled.

"What?" she asked.

"I know what you're thinking," he said dryly. "We're creating a story, remember?"

"I'd almost forgotten."

He ignored that. "I thought we could talk about your work a bit. You may have yourself some ready-made investors there. If it's too uncomfortable for you, though—"

"No…" Why did she sound so weak? "No," she said, and lifted her chin. "I am fine. I'm happy to play hostess."

"Good."

A muscle worked in his cheek. She heard him take a breath. And suddenly Kitty realized.

*He's as uncomfortable with this as I am.*

Instead of running from what made him uncomfortable, though, Laurence barreled toward it at full speed. Perhaps he was determined to prove that certain things did not affect him anymore.

Perhaps she should do the same.

She could not stay in the protective shell she'd buried herself in—not forever. It had been fine for healing, but she had to emerge eventually. She supposed, in a sense, that there was no better time than tonight...

In Kitty's memory, the Stones' Long Island mansion loomed as an example of the life she'd lost—a representation of the fact that things, beautiful things, could be snatched away in an instant and growing too attached to anything was a mistake.

The house was ensconced in the wilds of Long Island's North Shore, among the remnants of New York's old money: geriatric millionaires. It had been built in a cool hamlet off a turnpike lined so heavily by low-hanging trees that the private road was completely shrouded from view of oncoming drivers.

Laurence had sent his car for her, and she'd spent most of the hour-plus ride checking her makeup and trying to fight back a nervousness that manifested itself in a vaguely sickish feeling—the kind of feeling that came from keeping terror at bay.

The Stones had used the Georgian-style red-brick mansion as a summer home. It looked like it had been lifted from an illustration of a Fitzgerald novel, with the sun setting behind it, washing the grounds in peach-tinted light.

Inside, it was still decorated with the grave sort of opulence that seemed more appropriate for a museum—lots of leather, and dark wood paneling finished to a high polish. As she walked in the feeling of *déjà vu* grew even stronger; she recognized pictures, figurines, even the smell of the dust.

By the time she reached the study, and Laurence, Kitty had composed herself enough to offer a tentative smile. "I feel as if I'm trespassing."

"You're not the only one." Laurence crossed over to the wet bar. "Whisky?"

"Please." Funny how she'd developed a taste for it since going out with Laurence.

"Strange, isn't it?"

He was talking to her but not looking at her, palming two large whisky glasses and then setting them down, decanting amber liquid into the bottom of each. He looked almost grim.

"What is?"

"Being here."

He handed her a glass, then downed his own in one quick gesture. He looked at it, as if surprised by how quickly he'd drained it, then shook his head and placed it back on the bar.

"I never thought…"

Kitty's hands tightened round her glass involuntarily. "Never thought what?"

"Don't' worry about it." He cleared his throat. "I'm going to get dressed. Will you be all right?"

"Haven't got a choice now, do I?"

He smiled wryly and left.

Things happened very quickly after that. Laurence came back, devastatingly handsome in black cashmere and wool, and the Muellers arrived, apple soufflé in hand, full of cheer and bluster.

Laurence took Giles on a tour of the house, while Kitty obeyed Doris's very detailed instructions on how to unpack the delicate dessert and greeted the other guests as they arrived, ensuring that the wait staff kept the glasses filled and that the table for ten was set to perfection.

It felt oddly domestic, and the feeling only intensified as Laurence dismissed the servers, sharpened knives and took to the enormous juicy roast himself, piling their plates high. Kitty caught his eye once, as she was refilling water glasses from the crystal pitcher on the table. She had to turn a laugh into a cough when he wiggled his brows.

Laurence had prepared for this so much. Had arranged the homey setting, right down to the steaming roast and the potatoes, and him with his sleeves pushed up; Kitty in her gifted finery; the beautiful mansion on Long Island; the roaring fire; the conversation; the laughter.

None of it was real. It was intended to manipulate a man into signing a deal. And if Laurence could do this for mere business, what was he capable of in other areas?

A chill wafted round the table and she shivered. She'd forgotten how cold this house could be. Laurence saw her and stood up, tugging off his blazer and draping it round her shoulders. She nosed at the soft fabric, which was a mistake; her senses were immediately overcome by soap, spice, the barest hint of custom-mixed cologne.

"I forgot to tell you it'd be cold," he said, his voice low and intimate, and he smoothed the wool down her arms before straightening up.

Everyone was smiling indulgently, and Kitty was suddenly *too* warm.

"I'm fine," she managed.

"Adorable…" Doris simpered.

Kitty could not have responded even if she'd wanted to; her senses were completely overwhelmed by the nearness of Laurence and those enormous hands resting heavy on her shoulders, by the memory of the kisses they'd shared after dinner only days ago. Her heart was heavy, too, with the realization that this—all of this—was part of the charade.

On an impulse, Kitty reached up and caught his hands in hers. The angle was awkward, so she only held them for a moment, but— Well… She wanted him to look at her. *Notice* her the way he hadn't since that night. Do something unscripted, even if it was just for that minute.

"Thank you, Laurence," she said. She tipped her head back, smiled—and let go of his hands.

A muscle worked in his jaw, but he said nothing. Doris and Giles chatted inanely. Her head hurt, and not just from tiredness. The memories were coming now, hard and fast. She wanted the dinner to be over—desperately.

She was almost there, she told herself. Giles was stacking plates in a jolly manner and handing them off to the silent server who stood in the wings. Plates of apple soufflé with piles of fresh whipping cream and apple cinnamon sauce were being passed round to guests who were exclaiming that they were *much* too full but eating it anyway.

Kitty stared at the pools of cinnamon and cream melting into each other, feeling rather dazed, and she jumped when Laurence jabbed her with his foot.

*Talk*, he mouthed, shooting daggers across the table.

Kitty felt a rush of anger that compressed her lungs so that speaking was impossible.

*I should have never come here.*

It had been a severe miscalculation, thinking she could handle this foray back into her past. Nothing superseded Laurence's need to win— and he'd never regard her feelings any more than his parents had.

"Are you quite all right, dear?" Doris was saying kindly.

Kitty managed somehow to make her lips move. "I'm well," she said, and he heard Laurence exhale. "I was in state care for some time, as you know, and I spent some time in a house in this very neighborhood."

She saw Laurence's face blanch. *Good.* He'd wanted her to *talk*, hadn't he?

"Did you really?"

Kitty nodded. "It was the inspiration for my

foundation," she explained, and took a sip of wine to wet her tongue.

Laurence looked absolutely furious, but he needn't worry; she didn't have it in her to air the details of her past just to spite him.

"So many people of means have resources they can use to help—and would if they knew how to. Sponsorship is an easy way to do good and still ensure the young people remain independent. Even the most successful people in the world—" and here she dared a glance at Laurence "—got help to start up in life, whether it was money, connections, or education. I want to help my young people with the first."

The Muellers were both nodding, as were the other guests. Laurence's face was unreadable.

"She's done a tremendous amount of good work so far," he said flatly.

The couple asked a few more questions, and conversation, dessert and coffee continued for another hour. After much effusive thanks, and a promise to see Laurence in the morning to iron out the paperwork, they left with much fanfare.

The two of them saw the rest of the group off, waving woodenly until the last car disappeared down the road, taillights dancing.

Without looking at her, Laurence turned and

went back inside. Kitty's jaw dropped. She hurried behind him, closing the heavy door. Aside from the catering service, clearing up in the kitchen, the place was very quiet.

"Laurence!"

"Your ride will be here in twenty minutes," Laurence said tonelessly. "Should have been here twenty minutes ago, actually. I should fire that man."

"Are you not going to talk about—?" Kitty began.

But Laurence turned in a moment of fury that had Kitty shrinking back against the wall of the foyer. She felt his wool dinner jacket sliding off her shoulders, but she could not pull herself away from his expression to bend and pick it up. His eyes were *blazing*.

"Just what the *hell* did you mean with that line about my getting help to start up in life?"

Kitty was flummoxed. "What line—?"

"Don't deny it was a hit at me. You, Katherine Asare, know nothing about me." He spat out every word, a dark fury on his face. "I worked hard for everything I have, and I wouldn't take a penny from them. I've built everything I've done from the ground up."

Kitty laughed. She couldn't help it. The idea

of what he was claiming was too absurd. "What, with your prep school education, your billionaire business partner and your trust funds?"

"I paid back every penny I took out of my—"

"Yes, but it was and is still there, isn't it? Any bank would give you any amount of money based on the fact that they exist. You didn't have to spend years building your credit and still get rejected. You didn't have to pour personal funds into your business and risk starvation otherwise. Even your motive for signing the Muellers—" Kitty's lip curled upwards. "The pretense makes me sick. It'll benefit both of you. You live *nothing* like the rest of us!"

Laurence had closed the distance between them and Kitty felt fear, but it wasn't fear that he'd hurt her. She knew Laurence was not capable of real violence. It was fear of his closeness, fear of what the stormy look on his face heralded, fear of whatever he was about to say. He looked for the first time since he'd come back into her life like the stormy-faced teen she remembered, angry and resentful.

She dared not touch him. The heat emanating from his body at these close quarters hinted at things she could not want, now or ever, despite what had happened between them only days ago.

Her mind conjured up an unfortunately vivid recollection of the two of them only days before, in that trailer. Her dress and his big hands had been sliding torturously slowly up her thighs and then his fingers had been inside her, buried in her to the knuckle—

She cleared her throat, willing the images that were coming to disappear. "Laurence—"

He shook his head. "You've made your point," he said, and turned to head back down the hallway, leaving Kitty shivering.

She bent to pick up the soft black wool from where she'd dropped it on the ground and went after him. "Laurence!"

He paused, though he didn't turn around.

"I'm sorry." It nearly choked her to say it, but she could not ignore the fact that... Well, this evening must have been as hard for him as it was for her. "I shouldn't— You can't help what you were or what you had. It was unfair."

"You did nothing, Kitty." He wasn't looking at her face.

"We were children," she said, and at that Laurence actually flinched.

"Yes," was all he said, but his face was a study.

Kitty's heart was hammering with much more than adrenaline; it was suspicion. Suspicion that made her suddenly feel sick. Suspicion that she was on the precipice of a truth that quite possibly would shatter everything she'd thought was true up until this point.

He turned around and his face was still.

"Do you—?" She swallowed hard. "Do you know why they sent me away?"

She had never seen such a change in a man before. There was a look of absolute despair on his face. It flitted across it so quickly she might have missed it if she'd blinked, but she hadn't, and it made the stoniness that replaced it completely irrelevant.

She'd seen the real Laurence Stone, if only for a fraction, and it aroused something powerful within her, pushing fear into the background.

"Laurence?" she whispered, and stepped forward, resting her hands on his arms.

The muscles there were iron-tense, as was the rest of his body.

He had to get out of here.

Kitty hadn't said another word, and he'd turned, forced himself to walk normally into the study, putting one foot in front of the other.

Now he went to the decanter, poured a couple of fingers of amber liquid into a clean glass, held it out without looking. He knew Kitty would have followed him.

"I don't want a drink." Her voice was tremulous but decided. "You shouldn't have one either. It's silly, running for the bar whenever you hear something you don't like."

"This was a mistake," he said finally. "All of it was."

He'd managed to convince himself that the past didn't matter, that he could be ruthless enough to place emotion aside and concentrate solely on what both of them could get. He'd also managed to convince himself that making sure Kitty Asare succeeded in life was enough to make up for what had happened to her.

He tipped the contents of the glass into his mouth, barely registered as they went down his throat with smoky dark heat.

"Are you really not going to look at me?" she demanded.

He turned, facing the reason for the guilt that had been eating at him all evening head-on. Her lovely face was tight with anxiety and she was twisting her hands in her skirt, in that nervous habit he remembered from the races.

"Are we going to talk about this?"

"No. No, we are not."

He was itching to leave the room, to pace in privacy until he'd managed to push down the feelings Kitty had aroused, back into the deep dark places from where they'd come.

"You brought me back to this house, Laurence," she said, and her voice cracked painfully.

Laurence felt something deep inside himself rend in two as well.

"You brought me *back* here."

"Kitty..." He could see tears slipping down the soft skin of her face, making damp rivulets. He took a step toward her, but she shook her head violently.

"Do you know what happened the day I left?" She took a shuddering breath. "My case worker picked me up from school and told me I was no longer welcome, Laurence. I couldn't even pack my own things. She told me I was being 'reassigned,' as if I was working for a temp agency."

Bitterness colored her voice for the first time since he'd met her. "I was seventeen, and I had no idea what the hell I'd done that would possibly make your father—" She stopped. "I don't know," she repeated. "I don't know..."

"It wasn't you." Laurence's tongue felt heavy, swollen, stupid, and the roast in his stomach was congealing into something rather unpleasant. "It wasn't you. They—aren't good people."

He swallowed hard and then he reached out, touched her cheek. If he'd had any doubts about her motives now, they were quickly dissipating. Not because of the tears—mere tears would never move him. It was the fact that this woman… this beautiful, poised young woman…had come through the same home he had and had been wounded by the same people.

However, unlike him, she'd become better for it.

"You shouldn't cry," he said, and his voice was rough. "It isn't worth it. None of this is worth it."

"I know." She swiped furtively at her cheeks and peered up at him, ran a small pink tongue over lips that were already wet, swollen and, he knew from experience, plush and warm.

The sudden rush of awareness in his body had little to do with lust and everything to do with tenderness, and that startled him. It sparked an ache in his chest that was as uncomfortable as it was unexpected. He wanted her close, and if the way she was breathing was any indication she wanted that as well.

"This makes absolutely no sense," he said, and

he meant every word. However, his body relaxed, closing the final few inches between them.

"I know," she answered.

Kitty's slim fingers crept toward the cashmere covering his chest. He did not move, even though he knew that, by God, he should! She slowly, tentatively, pressed one knee up between his legs. He bit back a groan.

"Please take me to bed," she whispered, and it was those words, a little broken and a little defeated-sounding, that did it.

Laurence slid his hands round to her backside, drew her close so that the inches between them evaporated like smoke.

Kitty lifted her chin and looked into his face. "The past doesn't have to matter," she said. "Not tonight. And maybe if we finally..."

Her voice trailed off, but he knew exactly what she meant. Maybe if they had sex, if they finally allowed to happen what had been building for weeks, they'd finally be able to not want it anymore, in anticipation of when they went their separate ways.

A muscle jerked tight in Laurence's cheek, making his jaw go rigid. His mouth moved soundlessly for a moment, and he inhaled deeply before he spoke.

"It does," he said roughly. "It *does* have to matter. Because, Kitty, it was my fault they sent you away."

## CHAPTER TWELVE

WHEN KITTY BURST OUT from beyond the immediate circle of the Stones' mansion she found herself shrouded in darkness. It was a thick, choking darkness that was nothing like night in the city—a velvety blackness that completely engulfed everything around it.

She cried out, involuntarily, and clapped her hand to her mouth. She couldn't hear a thing over the blood drumming in her ears.

This was a nightmare—a nightmare akin to finding oneself naked and exposed to the elements—and memories assaulted her as well, hard and swift.

The first few nights after she'd been sent away were sharpest in her mind. She'd been scared half out of her mind, unsure of where she'd sleep, being bounced from house to house as Anna had looked for a room for her.

For nearly a year she'd cried herself to sleep every night, and all because—

She screamed again, in terror this time, when she felt someone reach out in the darkness and grab her from behind. She knew before the scream left her throat that it was Laurence, and she whirled around blindly, struck out at him with her fists.

"Don't you dare touch me!"

"Shh…" he said, and his voice rumbled low in his throat. There was no mocking there, and more than a little concern. "Kitty, you ran out—"

"Because I wanted to get away from you!"

"Out *here?* We're on six acres, Kitty. Where were you planning to go?"

"I'll call an Uber!"

He laughed incredulously, and Kitty felt a hatred for him so violent she wondered if she'd be sick. She attempted to shove him away. He wouldn't let her.

"Kitty, don't be an idiot. At least let me take you home."

"I don't want anything from you!" she shouted, and to her own self-disgust tears began to run down her face, hot and quick.

She had no idea why she was being so emotional after Laurence's admission. All she knew was that she had to get away from him, from this hideous portal to a past she'd tried so hard to forget.

"You're shaking," he said, and the note of wonder, of compassion, in his voice was almost too much.

Kitty fumbled for her phone, finally locating it in the innermost recesses of the handbag she thankfully hadn't forgotten, and activated the flashlight. It was surprisingly strong, illuminating them both in a watery but completely adequate beam of light.

"You're still *crying*." He said it almost accusingly.

"I tend to do that when I'm upset, yes," she said shortly, taking a full step back.

Laurence was holding out his hands as if to ward off something evil—or to tell her that he wasn't going to hurt her. Too late for both. She wiped furtively at her cheeks with her fists.

"Kitty—"

"You ruined my life, Laurence," she said, and her voice was shaking, too. "You *ruined* it for years. And you have the audacity to tell me—"

"I was *minutes* away from shucking up your skirt and taking you against that wall," Laurence said huskily, "and you would have let me. I wasn't going to do that without telling you."

Kitty half turned away from him, fisted her hands as tightly as she could and closed her eyes tight as well, as if she could banish him from her side merely by doing so. He did not disappear with the night; she could still hear him breathing.

"Kitty."

"Go away!"

He swore low, under his breath. "I'm not going to leave you here."

"You brought me here."

Kitty hated how small she sounded. She hated it more than anything.

The silence that followed was punctuated by her steady breaths and Laurence's deep ones, and then he spoke, his voice heavy with something unsaid.

"You don't know the whole story. I did you a favor, Kitty. *Trust* me. My parents—"

She saw the vague roundness that was his head shake, and heard his voice, low and urgent.

"Whatever happened to you—it was a blessing in disguise. Trust me. You're much better off without having—"

Kitty turned on him in a fury.

"Don't give me your 'poor little rich boy' schtick, I'm tired of it!" she cried. "You have *no idea* what it's like to— It wasn't about the money, you idiot. Anyone can make money. It was having *parents*, if only for a short time—parents who could do anything for me. I hadn't had anyone take care of me properly for years, and then your parents did—"

"Kitty—"

"You were a selfish little bastard. You *lied* and you made me lose that—"

Her voice did break then, despite her best efforts, and she pressed a hand to her mouth. Laurence was only a vague shape in front of her, and she was glad for it. It meant that she, too, would barely be more than a mass. He would not be able to see the tears that still slid down her face, see how devastated she really was. Reduced back to poor little orphan Katherine Asare, standing in a big house where she didn't belong, begging for someone—*anyone*—to love her.

She hated Laurence for bringing that back.

Kitty barely registered it when Laurence moved closer to her, lifted his arms, wrapped them round her shoulders.

"Don't touch me," she said feebly.

"I know," he said, more gently than she'd ever heard him say anything before.

But he did not break the embrace. He held her, not tightly, not loosely, but just enough for her to feel warm, secure, without feeling restrained. He held her as if he'd done it a million times before…as if he knew exactly how she liked to be held…and that made her want to cry harder.

To be comforted by this—*this*—

"Hate me if you want," he said, and his voice was rougher than it normally was, his breath soft and warm by her ear. "I likely deserve it."

"I don't think enough of you to hate you," Kitty said. Her nose and throat were clogged and her voice sounded odd, strangled, as she told the lie.

"Kitty…"

There was enough hesitation in his voice to give her pause. Coming out of the shadows, it sounded as unlike Laurence as it could—subdued, a little uncertain, with none of the sardonic dryness, none of the superiority.

His hands slid down to capture hers, as if helping her brace for a blow. "Listen. You were brought into my father's house deliberately."

"I know. Because of the campaign."

"No—no, sweetheart, it was more than that." He compressed his lips, then released them. "My father operated three sham charities, Kitty. *Three.* One that solicited cancer donations, one for education, and one—"

Kitty felt her heart drop like a stone. "One foster care program," she said dully, and he nodded.

"It was all in the records I leaked, but— I don't know... To this day, I'm not sure how he hushed the bulk of it up."

Kitty's head ached; she was finding it hard to follow. "So—what? You got me kicked out to *protect* me?"

He was quiet for so long that she drew back, looked up at his face. Even encased in shadow it was dark and troubled.

"I should have let you leave on your own terms. But I knew I was going to leak the documents, and I didn't trust you to leave. Your name would have been all over them. He was going to name the charity after *you*, Kitty."

Did he remember, then, the night he'd been so kind to her as they'd stood together under the lights of the chandelier in the grand ballroom of his parents' home? Did he realize how much his small attentions to her that night had meant? Had that, perhaps, led to this act of mercy, misguided as it was?

She'd never forgotten that moment of gentleness, and the memory had always had her telling herself that there had been at least one person in the Stone household who'd thought she was worth regard, even for a moment.

Now, faced with his lie, the memory of her gratitude was laced with humiliation. The Stones had cared nothing for her, and if Laurence had been kind to her that evening he'd had his own motives.

When her body had ceased its trembling Laurence pulled away from her, as if he wanted to steer them back to the house. She did not move. It was safer here in the dark and, if she was honest with herself, she did not want to leave the circle of his arms, despite her anger. The rage that had propelled her from the door had faded, leaving an ache in its place that was only heightened by the fact that not only *was* he close, he *felt* close.

"Kitty?" His voice rumbled out of the dark.

Kitty pressed her hands to her face, and it was a long moment before she spoke. "Why did you help me?" she said.

He exhaled. "The New Year's party."

Kitty's throat was so tight that she found it hard to speak. "You remember that night?"

"Every minute." He shifted from leg to leg. "Listen… I was kind of an ass of a kid, but after that night— You looked so uncomfortable. I wanted to get you away from what was going to happen. It's not great, having your name tied to people like them."

Laurence's words washed over her, but only two really stuck, reverberating in her head. *Every minute.*

*He remembered.*

The admission blossomed warm in her chest and she licked her lips. Wild emotion was quickly fading into something else entirely, and she shifted. She smelled that mixture of spice and whisky and soap and something else—some clean, masculine scent that was absolutely Laurence. Her skin began to prickle with awareness, and she suddenly felt more tired than she ever had in her life.

Why was she still even here?

"Kitty?" he asked, and she still couldn't speak.

She closed whatever little distance was left between them. Despite the silence it took her a moment to locate his heartbeat; it thudded strong and sure against her palm.

"I should have told you earlier," he said, and his voice was sober.

"Why didn't you?"

"I didn't want you to back out of the deal."

*The deal.*

The only thing that had brought them together.

Those two words pulled Kitty back to herself, though she didn't move. It didn't matter how fleetingly kind he'd been to her once upon a time, or how good it felt to be in his arms. He was still Laurence Stone, and he would always put himself first.

That realization did not change the fact, however, that he was still close, and that she ached for him now even more than before, if that was possible. If anything, this had added layers to it.

He let out a sigh, and she decided in a flash to be honest. It wasn't as if things could get any worse.

"I still want you," she said, and gulped. "How is that even possible?"

"I don't know," he said.

And apparently he could read her mind, because he was nosing her face in the darkness, skimming that spot on her neck that made her shiver, whispering words that made no sense, and then finally—much to her relief—capturing her lips with his.

Kitty braced her hands on his chest, fisting the cashmere in her fingers, venting her frustration in little whimpers against his lips. She wanted it hard and fast and urgent, matching the way her pulse was racing, but Laurence was kissing her with the gentle intimacy of a lover who knew he had the entire night before him.

His hands were making a leisurely exploration of her hips, her waist, threading through her hair. She arched her chest up to meet them, greedy for them. His large palm cupped her right breast—finally—and even through the layers of her bra and the fine wool his thumb had no trouble locating her thrusting, aching nipple circling it almost lazily, a whisper of a touch.

Just as she was soothed in the gentle rhythm he tugged, with just the right amount of pressure, and she cried out—a soft exhalation of pleasure this time.

"We can't do this here," he said, with a modicum of his old briskness, and Kitty squeezed her eyes shut.

He was right, of course. This business between the two of them was insanity in and of itself, but doing this here, with their past hovering round them in these halls like a malicious, disembodied spirit, was an entirely new level of *no*.

She shivered a little and he nodded, as if she'd confirmed something he had already been thinking.

"Come home with me," he said simply.

*"Why?"* she cried out.

He sighed. "Damned if I know."

She laughed—a short, shaky sound—and pushed her hair back over her shoulders. She couldn't have spoken even if she'd wanted to; she didn't trust her voice. Instead of walking, she reached out and took his hand, a little hesitantly. She felt such relief when his fingers closed over hers, warm and sure, that her heart seemed like it might burst in her chest.

Kissing Laurence Stone in a heated moment was one thing; giving him clearance to reject her was another. Knowing he wanted her, even if just physically, as much as she wanted him—

Two sides of her were warring now, but the need throbbing through her blood obliterated all reason. Once that fire had been doused, she thought a little hopelessly, perhaps she'd be able to think straight, to finally push Laurence Stone out of her life, precisely where he belonged.

"All right," she said quietly.

The moments after that were spent in the driveway, and then in the car, in a haze of heated kisses, frenzied groping, both alight with the frustration that came from not being able to get one's hands where one wanted them, *when* you wanted them. Laurence seemed intent on torturing her, on drawing out her want until she snapped.

When the car finally stopped he twisted away from her with great effort.

"Minx," he half growled, then took a deep breath before sliding out of the car, ahead of his driver, then going to open Kitty's door himself.

She ignored his hand and looked around instead in shock. "This is—"

"The harbor," he agreed, and began to walk toward the dock.

He'd only gone a few feet before he realized that Kitty was still peering out of the car, shivering in her thin evening dress.

"What are you doing?"

"I'm not following you. You said we were going to your place."

It took Laurence a moment to get it; then he began laughing uproariously.

"I live on a boat," he said, still chuckling. "I'm not planning to tie you to bricks and pitch you in the Hudson. Come on, Kitty."

"You live on…a *boat*?"

"Sometimes, yes."

Kitty was thunderstruck.

Laurence wrapped an arm around her as protection from the wind, and began to hustle her down the pier. When they reached a small motorboat with a man silently waiting inside, Laurence pointed into the gray mist on the horizon.

"There," he said, indicating a looming shape not far off the coast. "This is as far as they let me come in, usually. New York is fairly crowded; it'll take us about forty minutes to get there."

"What do you do during the winter?" Kitty demanded as he lifted her down, then swung himself over expertly and draped a soft waterproof blanket over her shoulders.

He huddled next to her. "I have a suite at the Plaza."

She could see him smile, even in the dim light.

"And all the room service you could want."

She reached out to hit his arm; he caught her and drew her close.

"You're lucky I don't get seasick," she murmured, then sighed a little as their lips met again, stoking her desire even more.

It felt unearthly now, as if they'd transported themselves to their own little dimension, where nothing mattered but being *alone*.

They could not be alone, though—not yet. She had to be welcomed aboard the massive yacht by a staff of thirty. She had to watch Laurence and the housekeeper, who greeted him with the deference due to the young master, had to watch him wave off the transport boat, muscles straining against the cotton confines of his sweater, had to hear about what food was in the fridge and what rooms had been prepared for them, then see the housekeeper off into the muggy damp of the night.

Kitty was so desperate for him by the time he'd finished that she was biting her lip raw.

"Let's go," he said, and then they were in an elevator, going below the main deck.

When the gilt doors closed her throat was dry as sandpaper and dampness was trickling down between her breasts, between her legs… She closed her eyes.

In one single movement Laurence wrapped her in his arms from behind and his hands were suddenly everywhere: cupping her backside, on her breasts. One rough, insistent hand was going further, parting her thighs…

Kitty came so fast she had no time to make a sound. There was little build-up—just the gentle stroke of blunt fingers between her folds before it overcame her, a fitting end to the tension of the past hour. She bent over, her skirt hitched to her waist, panting. She could feel the hard length of him against her backside, and barely had enough time to gain her bearings before he turned her around, kissed her hard.

"Now," she said, and her voice was a whimper.

"You must think I'm way more dexterous than I actually am," he said, and his voice was rough, his words disjointed.

"Laurence, *please*."

When he moved as if to exit the elevator she shook her head and backed up.

"Here," she said quietly, and leaned back against the wood-paneled wall.

His eyes darkened; she squeezed her own shut.

She had to do it this way to ensure that whatever happened between them remained meaningless, without the tenderness that would rope her heart into it. In a moment she heard foil tear, and arched her back as he hoisted her up. Then she was against the wall, the flimsy mesh of her underwear was wrenched to the side, and he was *finally* inside her.

"Kitty…" he groaned, and her answer was to dig her nails into his back as hard as she could.

She'd only had one partner before this—a sweet but bland boy in college who'd left her feeling decidedly indifferent. She'd never experienced the wild wanting that she did for this man who held her in his arms now. Not even close.

Laurence's breath was hot on her neck with an urgency she knew he rarely let show. There was a broken, "Please, sweetheart, *please*," and increasingly ragged breaths.

Kitty wrapped a leg round his waist, clutched him hard, and against all odds, against everything that made sense, she felt another orgasm coming—yes, there it was!

They sagged against the wall together, Kitty with her dress bunched round her waist, limp and useless, Laurence with his trousers unfastened but otherwise dressed.

There were a few moments before Laurence's hand crept out, searching, tugging her to him. He wrapped his arms round her, held her close. "It shouldn't have been like this," he said, and his voice was ragged.

If she hadn't known him better she would have guessed that was actually emotion leaching through.

"Not the first time. Not *tonight*, Kitty—"

"I wanted it," she said softly, tracing a finger down his back.

She felt his muscles tighten and pulse in response, and then he released her, leaving her cold, bereft.

"Excuse me. I'm sorry. I'll be back in just a

moment," he said roughly, and exited the elevator, doing up his trousers as he left and leaving her in a heap on the tiled floor.

He made it only a few feet before he stopped.

He just had to *breathe*.

It would serve him right, Laurence thought grimly, trying vainly to calm himself down, if he had a panic attack right at this moment.

Adrenaline was still coursing through him, making him shake, and his body had yet to come down from the high of taking Kitty Asare here, in the one place he used to escape from the world and all its ills.

His chest still ached with a longing that his climax had done nothing to assuage and, worse than that, guilt weighed heavy on him too—a guilt that made his stomach churn and his head ache.

He wished he'd never touched her.

He wished—

"Laurence?"

Kitty was behind him. He turned. He hadn't made it very far from the elevator, just halfway down the cream and gold tiled hallway that led to his stateroom. He didn't answer; if he did he might be sick. Instead he turned and glared.

She crept over in her bare feet, her shoes in her hand. "Are you all right?" she asked, and for once he felt the stone facade he kept round himself begin to shift.

Each time Kitty spoke to him he felt like it cracked a little more—as if she were a light that shone beyond it, to the parts of him he kept hidden from everybody else. Maybe it was because she'd witnessed him at his lowest, before he'd amassed all this, but it was there.

"This is wrong," he muttered, and Kitty's face changed.

She placed her shoes on the floor and approached him. There was a moment of hesitation before she lifted her arms to encircle his neck. "You'll drive yourself mad," she said quietly, "trying to figure out why things happened. You're not your parents—you are Laurence Stone. And I came here because I wanted to be with *you*."

Hell, that was taking the knife and twisting it in.

"You said you weren't cynical, but I didn't think you were stupid," he said.

"I haven't—" She stopped, started again. "I've only been with one other person, Laurence. I don't *do* this. I wanted you."

*What?*

Shock tightened his chest, but then he remembered Kitty's trembling hands, and the wordless way she'd come undone in his arms, and knew it was true. Her response wasn't that of an experienced lover.

He should end this here, take her back to shore, communicate with her neutrally until they both got what they wanted and then he could leave, knowing that although he'd ruined her life in some ways, he'd set her up for life in others.

*Kitty was his responsibility, whether she wanted to be or not, and knowing that—*

He licked his lips to moisten them before he spoke. "We can talk in the morning."

"We have work in the morning," Kitty protested.

But she was melting into him, and he allowed himself a kiss…her mouth was simply too alluring. Kissing her was like getting drunk: each sip made you thirstier for more. Telling her his secret had unleashed something in him, a freedom to finally take what he wanted from her.

"*You* have work in the morning," he husked, "and your work for the moment is to let me help you. Part of the deal, remember? I can do that from anywhere. *Stay.*"

Back in control, he let his fingers find the zipper at the back of her dress. She did not resist when he tugged it down, nor when he pushed the fabric from her shoulders to reveal smooth, butter-soft skin.

"I have donors to court."

"We can fly them out here."

"You have problems…" Kitty gasped.

But Laurence's attention was on the gleaming flesh revealed by the relatively demure dress, and, *dear God*—

"Were you hiding these from me the whole time?" he murmured.

Her breasts were full and high, tightly restrained by lace and the softest silk he'd ever felt. The flimsy clasps opened easily, and he made a low sound deep in his throat as she spilled into his hands.

"They were right there the whole time," she said archly, although she was doing nothing to stop her dress's journey to the ground.

Laurence was completely lost in sensation, in taste, in the want that had consumed him since he'd laid eyes on her in the Park Hotel's dining room. His fingers slid up to her hair, catching in the soft waves. She made a little sound of protest, but he kissed the smooth, vulnerable column of her throat.

"Don't worry, I won't pull your extensions out," he said, allowing himself a laugh. *Yet.* "Will you stay?"

"Laurence—"

Inexplicably, he was near ready for her again, his body surging with desire. Kitty's naked form was so incredibly womanly, even in its slenderness, and the way she submitted to his touch inflamed him all the more. She was so very innocent, he thought, but in some ways she had the mind of a hardened cynic.

"Let me do this for you," he whispered. "I'd like to make love to you properly. *Please.*"

It was that word on his lips that did it. Kitty met his gaze with uncertain eyes, but she nodded.

"Room," he said, a little unsteady. "Behind you. And don't rush me this time."

Once inside his suite, Laurence brushed her cheek with the backs of his fingers; he couldn't help it. Her skin was soft and warm, and so very inviting. Tonight he was selfish enough to indulge the want that pooled low in his belly without thought, without reservation. Tomorrow he would think about the practicalities.

His hands were her on her thighs, on her firm round backside, and she was gasping soft and sweet against his mouth between kisses…

By the time they'd stumbled over the threshold Kitty had been shivering, even in the warmth of his entryway. Now, with the bedroom door closed, he slid his hands up the cool smoothness of her thighs to her waist.

"Help me with my shirt," he said.

The first two buttons were slow, undone with fumbling, hurried fingers. When his neck was bare she kissed it, a whisper-soft contact on warm skin. She let her lips linger for a moment as she steadied herself.

The intimacy of the touch was not lost on Laurence, but he allowed her soft, full mouth to skitter across his skin as she uncovered more. A small part of him was touched by the care she was taking. It was more than a technique to arouse him…she had a tenderness that was elemental, part of her being.

When she reached the hard, flat plane of his belly he reached down and caught her wrists in his hands. She looked up, confused and a little anxious, peering up at him through a curtain of glossy dark hair.

"You *never* want me to touch you," she said, a little accusingly.

"I'm not very good at that," he admitted. "Come to bed." His voice was hoarse.

In response she wrapped her arms round his waist and burrowed into the warm expanse of bare skin she had been kissing just moments before.

"Okay," she said, muffled against him.

He tucked her close to his side before he began the short walk to his bed, and lifted her fingers to his lips.

Laurence made her wait…made her work for it.

He held her in place with one rigid hand on her hip, teasing her with his fingers, showing her the best angle, watching her strain downwards with eyes that he knew had darkened with wanting. There wasn't any letting up on that swollen bud between her nether lips. When she bit her lip and spread her thighs wider, begging soundlessly, he gave her one finger, then two, then three.

He wanted her feverish, frantic. But when her walls locked on his fingers tight and drew him in, he nearly lost control himself. He loved the way she trembled. It was with desire, and a desire that belonged to him and no one else.

When she was at the precipice he slowly withdrew his fingers, ignored her whimper of protest, cupped her instead. He twisted silk and lace with his fingertips, tugging it up to rub against where she wanted it the most. He told her in a soft, husky murmur that he was going to wrench those panties right off her, but she had to *tell* him to.

"I—" She couldn't say it; she was biting her lip, instead.

He loved the way her face strained when she talked, as if passion forced the words from her despite her natural reticence. And the fact that he already loved something about her was disconcerting, but not surprising.

He rubbed one thumb slowly over the dusky nipples jutting out from smooth skin, followed it with a gentle scrape of his teeth. The other hand drifted down to where she was wet, swollen, ready for him. Again, she made attempts to touch him, to reciprocate, but he didn't let her. He waited until she was shuddering against his hand before his first thrust, and he was grateful for that, for he did not last long himself.

When Kitty finally slept, snuggled trustingly

against his chest, Laurence looked at her face for a moment, more troubled than he'd been in years. He brushed her hair back and kissed her on the forehead before easing out of her embrace carefully. She was so lovely in sleep, and he couldn't look at her without feeling a palpable tug. His mind kept going back to their confrontation outside the Stone mansion, and in an instant he knew why he cared so much.

Laurence never wanted to see her cry again. *Never.* Whether she was angry with him, or pleased, or amused, he wanted her happy. *Fulfilled.*

Those cracks in the stone wall of his inner self had widened to proper gaps now, and Kitty had eased herself in. She was prickly and sweet and strong and kind, so unlike him, and he was transfixed.

Life had shown him to distrust love; he'd only ever seen it come with strings. Kitty's dedication to helping people was one thing; her coming here with him was another. She didn't despise him for what he'd done…she'd pushed her own pain aside to let him in, even if only for a night.

*She deserves everything.*

Laurence needed to open his computer, sit down, *plan.* Take some action. He could not give

Kitty back what she'd lost, and he couldn't re-write the past. He could, however, ensure her future was secure—and he would, long before they disembarked!

Barefoot, Laurence crept out to the study adjacent to his suite. His mind was now remarkably clear, and his body hummed with purpose. He messaged Cordelia, warning her that he'd need her in ten minutes. There were people to call, properties to acquire, things to set in place.

Before the end of the week, One Step Ahead would be a trailblazer in its field and Kitty would finally be able to bury the demons that plagued them both.

He refused to think about what this might mean for them, or if there even *was* a "them." Considering that was like icy fingers around his neck. If he cared for Kitty…if he cared for her at all—

Laurence closed his eyes, took a deep breath, tried his damnedest not to think of the woman asleep next door, or how badly he wanted to go back to that bed, draw her into his arms again. This would be a fine distraction. It would be folly, with their history, to think they could ever be more than this, and he had to leave her with something to make up for their inevitable separation.

If he could think of Kitty as a problem that needed solving, rather than a woman he was growing to care about, he'd never be put in the position of hurting her again.

Kitty did not trust him, and he couldn't blame her.

He didn't trust himself.

# CHAPTER THIRTEEN

KITTY FOUND HERSELF tangled in the Egyptian cotton sheets that covered Laurence's enormous bed when she woke up. She was stark naked and completely disheveled; he was nowhere to be found. She tumbled out of bed and hurried to the portholes that looked out to the sea. All she could see was watery gray, and she pressed her hands against her mouth, stifling a gasp.

He'd kidnapped her!

In disbelief Kitty reeled back, then scrambled over to the bed, looking for her clothes. She saw nothing but her lace underwear, tangled in the sheets, close to the foot of the bed.

"Good morning."

At the sound of Laurence's voice, lazy and languid, Kitty nearly fell. She recovered quickly and whirled around. Inexplicably, he looked as if he'd woken up from a full night's rest. His eyes were clear and bright, and he was dressed in a much more casual version of his usual office wear, a slim-cut cuffed linen shirt with matching trousers.

She drew the sheet tight over her breasts, embarrassed by her own dishabille. "Laurence, where are we?"

He squinted at the tablet in his hand. "The Atlantic."

Kitty felt very much as if she'd been turned unexpectedly on her head. "We're at *sea*?"

"Since a couple of hours after we got on board." His mouth twisted up into a mocking shape. "You didn't even notice when we started moving."

Kitty's face flamed. "I *did* notice!"

"Well, you didn't protest."

No, she hadn't—because he'd had her very distracted at that particular time. But she forced herself not to go down that road. "Laurence…" she began, in her most no-nonsense voice.

"I did say we'd work from here for a few days, didn't I?" he added, then cast an eye over her. "I've been up since five-thirty and have had coffee already. But you can eat breakfast with me if you can shower and be dressed quickly. We can talk over our schedule. I've got an investment opportunity for you—"

At this point Kitty was gaping. She'd never

seen him this way. His face was bright with an eagerness, an *energy* she'd never seen before.

"Anyway. I'll bring you up to speed as soon as you're ready."

Kitty looped up the hem of the bedsheet and began to walk rapidly, then broke into a run. She'd had no idea a man that size could move so quickly outside of a sports setting.

"Laurence—listen to me! You'll take me back to New York this minute—"

"We already talked about that."

"We didn't *talk* about anything!" Kitty panted. "I don't even have a current passport, for one thing."

"A yacht is a floating country, Kitty," he said in that patronizing voice she hated. "Send your details over and I'll have Cordelia sort it out. She'll have it waiting at the next port of call. Anything else?"

*Port of call?*

Kitty felt an urge to laugh, despite her anger. This was like a two-person cruise from hell.

Laurence stopped abruptly at the door, and Kitty plowed directly into his back. She swore and took a full step back, almost losing her hold on the sheet.

Laurence's eyebrows climbed as he turned around. "Why don't you get dressed?"

"My clothes are—"

And here, Kitty's face flamed. Her dress was on the back of an antique desk chair in his sitting room, where he'd unzipped her out of it so skillfully. The thin lace scrap of her bra was on the floor in the doorway, and she knew her lace underwear, damp from his skillful tongue and her own wetness, lay tangled in his sheets.

Laurence's brows lifted, as if he'd been reading her mind during this audit, and his chuckle made her spark with indignation.

"Do you need a moment?" he drawled.

"Oh—you—!" She stalked past him, throwing the sheet from her body rather dramatically, she knew.

She could feel him smiling, even though she could not see his face, and she was not afraid when she felt the hardness of his body press against her naked back. In fact, she sighed, felt her body relax.

His arms went around her and he kissed her neck. "You smell *delicious*," he said, and there it was: desire curling low in her belly.

There was a lightness in his voice that hadn't been there the night before. It was as if he'd exorcised something in the night, left it at the shore they'd sailed from.

"I smell like I've been out for twenty-four hours without changing my clothes," she said sulkily, trying not to shiver at the feel of his lips on her skin. "I want to bathe. And I want to get dressed."

"Just go with it, Katherine," he said, and there it was again, that hair-fine tension sparked by his voice caressing the vowels of her full name.

His big hands slid up her stomach, over her ribs, pausing to cup her breasts. They felt heavy and hot from their previous coupling, and so very sensitive. When his thumb circled the swollen bud of her left nipple her breath manifested itself in a stuttered gasp. When he pinched it none-too-gently she nearly lost her feet.

"Laurence…" she murmured.

"One more go?" he asked, as if he were asking if she wanted another helping of food.

His hand had left her breast and was descending to where her thighs pressed hard together. His fingers danced over her mound as if toying with the idea of her, and Kitty hesitated for a fraction of a second before rolling her hips, so that her backside was pressed directly into the cradle of his thighs.

"Is that a yes?"

He found her aching bud with gentle fingertips, using one digit to press before circling slowly— too slowly. His lips descended to her ear and Kitty couldn't have stopped squirming even if she'd wanted to, for he was telling her things, low and filthy in her ear…things he wanted to do to her that he hadn't before. But there was no time, because if he didn't have her that minute he was going to spend himself right here on her skin.

Kitty was so dazed by lust that she could do little but lick her lips, focusing on the sound of foil tearing, on how gentle he was when he finally lowered her to her hands and knees.

"Okay?" he asked, probing her quivering wet sheath from behind.

She heard a groan as her walls clamped hard against his exploring fingers. She wasn't sure if it was him or herself.

"You're so ready."

"Do it," she panted.

She was past dignity now—all she wanted was for him to fill her completely, to answer the need her body was screaming for.

"Or is that a you'll see?" he said, amusement coloring his voice.

She could feel the tip of him at her entrance.

She strained backwards but he held her hips fast with one hand, while the other still circled the little bud between her thighs, almost idly.

Kitty almost cried in frustration. "You're insane!"

"Yes," he agreed. And then they both gasped, for he'd pushed completely inside her. Kitty felt her body soften, spasm, draw him in. "That doesn't affect this, though—"

Kitty began to laugh. She couldn't help it. Her laughter, though, was soon lost to husky breaths as he began to move, and then there was no sound in the room but that of skin rasping on skin.

Kitty had to bite back her moans. This was good, yes—the best she'd ever had, to be honest…not that she'd much experience to fall back on. It felt amazing to stop thinking, to finally drop her pretensions, her worries, and just—

Laurence breathed out something she couldn't hear, and then his fingers twisted, *just so*, and she let out a cry that she was sure he'd hold over her later. She pitched forward. He caught her just in time, cradling her to his chest for a fraction of a moment before lowering her to the rug. She took a moment just to breathe, trying to acquaint herself with the wanton stranger who was lying, panting, outside of Kitty Asare's body.

He quickly eased himself off her, rolling onto his back. Kitty lifted her head just enough to look at him. "Did you—?" she began, then bit her lip, suddenly shy. Her own climax had left her shattered, so absolutely *weak*.

His lips twisted up. "How considerate of you," he mocked, but it was good-natured. "Yes. I did. A little more quietly than you, but I did."

Kitty wanted to tell him to shut up, but she closed her eyes and let her head drop instead. The lush, soft wool of the carpet felt absolutely and welcomingly soft right now. Her lashes fluttered shut.

"Breakfast?" he said.

"Breakfast," she mumbled.

Laurence's yacht, the *Triumph*, was opulent in a way so gloriously over the top that new surprises seemed to appear each time she crossed the deck. Kitty found it fascinating, and had spent the first few minutes after she'd left Laurence's quarters walking after a blank-faced member of staff, her shoes in her hand, bundled up in an enormous dressing gown.

She was uncomfortable and, she supposed,

none-too-fresh, but there was something curiously intimate about his scent on her skin. It hung around her in a gentle cloud after last night and this morning, tinted by the soft musk of sex. She felt marked, in a way, and was a little discomfited to discover that it did not bother her at all.

"Mr. Laurence said you're to have the Rose Room, miss," her escort informed her.

*Whatever that meant.*

"I'm very grateful," Kitty said, dryly.

"I'm to give you a quick tour as well," the woman said briskly.

The yacht was decorated in minimalist elegant shades of gold and cream, and its staterooms were all carefully planned and primed for dancing, dining, lounging, socializing. The top level featured a deck in hand-laid mosaic tiles, perfect for sunbathing, and there was a spa on the level below, complete with a full Moroccan bath tiled in white, coral, and the most brilliant blue Kitty had ever seen. An Olympic-sized saltwater pool took up a great deal of space on the main deck, hand-tiled with a scene that included a demon chasing a nymph.

Kitty clapped her hands when she saw it.

"It's a pain in the ass to clean," the woman

said. "Come on—I'll show you the interior, and then we'll go to your stateroom."

"The interior" was decorated in an old English style, with a library, an enormous dining room, and multiple staterooms—each decorated, the housekeeper explained, with a different theme. By the time they reached the Rose Room Kitty had dropped all pretense of indifference and her eyes were wide and delighted.

The massive stateroom had its own sitting area, full bathroom, a balcony and dining room, and was decorated in shades of blush, dusty rose, pearl-white, and the palest gray. Kitty's bare feet sank deep into a carpet so plush and soft it rivaled her best bedspread at home, and a massive arrangement of American beauties, the brightest colors in the room, filled the air with their sweet and heady scent.

She walked up to it, touched one of the petals with a finger. When would he have had the time to have flowers delivered, for goodness' sake?

"Have a nice stay here, miss," the woman said, interrupting her thoughts, then took the bag with Kitty's ruined dress in it. "Check the wardrobe. Mr. Laurence had a few things flown in for you this morning. Breakfast will be served on the Horizon Deck, one level up. Do ring if you need anything," she added with a rusty smile. "I'm Vera."

When she was gone Kitty crept into the bathroom, toying with the idea of showering instead of having a soak. Laurence was waiting for her, after all. Remembering how he'd all but kidnapped her, though, she rebelliously turned the taps to the hottest temperature she could stand and tipped half a jar of rose-and-vanilla-scented bath salts into the water.

She could use a soak. Their activities the night before and this morning had left her aching and sticky, in a guiltily pleasant way.

Half an hour later Kitty emerged from the Rose Room calm and fragrant, dressed in a cream sheath of the type of style and cut that she hadn't a prayer of affording, and flats that fit her perfectly. Her hair was pulled into a bun at the base of her neck; she'd touched gloss to her lips.

When Laurence saw her, his eyes became soft.

"I'm here to take you to breakfast," he said simply, then offered her an arm with an old-fashioned air that suited him very much.

When they were seated for breakfast, and Laurence had attacked a basket of bread, Kitty asked him about the yacht. "It's magnificent," she said.

"It's old," Laurence said.

It was just warm enough that they could eat together on the Horizon Deck, which featured a full bar where a server presided over mimosas and Bloody Marys and lifted silver lids off chafing dishes full of eggs, fresh fruit, and fresh bread so warm and fragrant that the smell lingered in the air long after it disappeared from their plates.

"World War II, I think. It's been refurbished several times—even been in a museum. I got it cheap, after graduation, mostly to piss the Senator off. It cost more to refurbish, even though it's not very big." He said that with a perfectly straight face. "Only a couple hundred feet."

Kitty chose to pass over that gem, and instead looked at him in curiosity. Over the few weeks they'd been involved he'd spoken very little about his past, or indeed about their shared history. Now, out in the balmy air of the open sea, he seemed more willing to talk.

As if he'd read her mind, Laurence looked up from his coffee and sighed. "What?"

Kitty felt her face grow hot. "I didn't—"

"You think it's strange that I live on the water?" he drawled.

"Well, it is a bit eccentric—"

"It's private," Laurence said, and his voice was

curiously flat. "Privacy wasn't something I got a lot of when I was a kid. Anyone who follows us out here—" he gestured widely "—would be seen from miles out. Enough time to hunker down, issue a gag order..."

"It's dumb," Kitty said decisively. "A man your age should have an actual place to live."

"I'll keep that in mind."

Kitty leaned back into the softness of her chair. It was padded in some woven fabric that felt like linen but was twice as soft. "What do we do now?" she asked.

His mouth tipped up and his eyes slid down the length of her...deliberately. "You haven't had enough?" he teased.

Her body instantly ran hot. "Laurence—"

"There are many more things I'd like to do to you, and there will be plenty of time for that," he said. with a hunger in his eyes that made her press her thighs together. "Do you have any idea how long I've wanted to get you alone, Katherine Asare?"

She had to get him off this trail of conversation, and fast.

She groped for the nearest thing. "I wanted to ask you something," she said. "Last night."

"Oh?"

There was a lilt in his voice that she did not care to explore, so she barged forward. "After—"

"After what?"

"After what you did." She took a sip of tea, mostly to hide her face. "And I left. What happened when your father found out?"

Laurence's face went still. He was quiet for so long that she thought he wouldn't answer, but then he spoke.

"I'll tell you because you asked. But no more after this, okay? Let's look to the future, Kitty, not at the past."

She nodded, and he continued.

His voice had quieted, but his words were clear, if clipped and short. To her, he sounded like the young people she served, when they were recounting painful memories. It was always done like this...in brief, staccato sentences designed to get across the most information in the quickest, least damaging way.

*Coping mechanism*, she thought, and sank her teeth into her lower lip as he went on. She did not want to interrupt him...not for any reason.

"After I leaked that stuff to the reporter..." He lifted his shoulders. "My biggest mistake was bragging that I'd done it, that something big was coming. I posted about it, and my father was livid, but he couldn't do anything—not with everyone's eyes on him. The media took the story…ran with it. I picked up followers on-line…the opposition took me on—as some sort of a mascot, I guess."

He laughed, and his eyes were suddenly very far away, as if he were looking at something well beyond the yacht they were on, far beyond the swaying of the waves.

"He managed to hush it up, of course, and make me look like a liar. I was in way over my head."

He was silent for a long time—so long that Kitty reached out and placed a hand on his arm. Partly to bring him back, partly because she simply wanted to touch him. His muscles were so taut that she winced, and he flinched, then blinked down at her.

The emotion that had flitted across his face was gone, replaced by that oddly stoic expression, the iron mask he pulled over his face, bolted shut at the edges. He looked at her as if he were trying to gauge something.

"I don't know," he said, with marked gentleness, "what it is about you that makes me want to talk."

Kitty tried to smile, but didn't quite manage it.

Laurence heaved a sigh, then took her hand, tugged her into his lap. It was as close a position as they could be in, and Kitty was faced with the disconcerting sensation of not knowing where her body ended and his began.

Laurence picked up his tablet, touched the screen. One swipe of his fingerprint and it was open, and he clicked on a series of files. His face was very still.

After a moment he handed it to her. "Take a look. Scroll down."

Kitty did so. The files held a series of scans of the pages of various newspapers: the *New York Times*, the *Journal*, the *Gazette*, the *Enquirer*. The headlines were in chronological order...

*Troubled Teen Laurence Stone Caught in Drug Bust!*

*Stone Jr. leaked doctored tax documents while "under the influence," Stone family lawyer says...*

*Troubled teen son of New York politician enters rehab; family despondent...*

Some headlines were more salacious than others, but they all told the same story. Laurence was at worst a manipulative liar, at best a troubled, drugged-up child worthy of pity rather than censure or admiration.

Kitty looked up, whispering the last one. "'*Stone Jr. enrolls at Sandhurst*'?"

Laurence nodded. "That was how it ended. It started when heroin was found in my bag," he said after a moment. "At an airport. Along with condoms and weed—that was a nice touch, and in a nice public place, with lots of witnesses. My father played the concerned parent to the max, of course. Shut down my social media accounts… suspended his…took some time off—enough to make sure I settled in well at what everyone assumed was rehab."

Kitty's stomach was twisting so violently it threatened to expel the breakfast she'd eaten. "The Senator did that to you?"

Laurence's mouth tipped up just a fraction. "I accused him of it. He told me I couldn't prove it—which was entirely correct. He also told me I was no longer welcome in his home. He informed me that he'd continue to pay for my schooling—he couldn't have the scandal of estrangement after all the tax nastiness."

Kitty pressed her hand to her mouth and Laurence shook his head, shifting her so that their foreheads were almost touching. His voice had a forced lightness that twisted her stomach even harder.

"No, sweetheart. Remember? I'm an ass and you hate me?"

"But that's horrible!"

"It was a long time ago." He lifted his shoulders. "I thought that the leak would exonerate me—but, Kitty, the man has connections everywhere. That journalist printed a retraction of his story within the week, saying I'd falsified the information I'd provided. Who knows what the Senator did to the man..."

"Oh, my God," whispered Kitty.

"It's politics. I was too young to know better." His mouth twisted, just a little. "I promised to never say a word about him to the media again if he'd send me as far away as possible."

"Sandhurst?"

"Yes. He paid to get me in, I'm sure."

"And then...?"

Laurence's broad shoulders barely moved. "Nothing. I graduated, went to uni, went into business with Desmond. Last contact I had with the Senator, I handed him a check that covered every single penny I'd taken out of my trust fund to start the firm. Paid him back for school, too."

"And he took it?"

"He did."

Kitty sagged back, suddenly overwhelmed, feeling slow and stupid. "I'm sorry," she whispered.

"Don't be sorry for me," he said, with all the arrogance she would normally despise—except now her heart ached not only for herself, but for him and what he'd become. "I'm fine now. So are you. Take everything you've got...be everything you've ever wanted to be, Kitty Asare. Use me while you've got me because nothing else matters. Love doesn't matter, Kitty. It won't stop people from putting themselves first. And it shouldn't. Take what you can and be unapologetic about it. The sooner you know that, the freer you'll be."

Kitty suddenly felt very tired. Why was she here, then, if Laurence didn't believe in love? More than that, why did she care if he didn't? What had she been hoping to get from this?

The possible answers were absolutely terrifying, and she instinctively placed some distance between them, wrapping her arms around herself.

"Laurence?" she said after a moment.

"Mmm...?"

Kitty swallowed. This was going to take all her courage, every bit of it, but Laurence had opened up. He'd shared things with her that she sensed he never had with anyone, and… Well, in her work she knew how difficult that was for a victim to do. She could not let that go—not without giving him something of her own.

In one quick motion she twisted and pressed her body flush against his. "You are a *good* man, Laurence Stone," she whispered fiercely. "I don't care how you try to come off. I know that with all my heart."

His response was extraordinary: shock, followed by a softness of expression that swilled the contents of her stomach violently.

"I—"

"I mean it," Kitty said firmly, swallowing the lump threatening to impede her speech. "I wouldn't have come here if I didn't think so. I *like* you. As yourself. I mean it."

"Oh." He blinked hard, once, and the fact that those simple words had affected him so much made Kitty a little misty-eyed herself.

"Don't look so shocked." She managed a smile. "Don't you believe me?"

Laurence coughed before he spoke, and Kitty

braced her hand on his cheek. He looked so different. Naked. Open. *Vulnerable.*

"I consider it a victory."

Kitty laughed a little awkwardly, and the two of them sat in silence for a moment, looking out over the sea. Then he cleared his throat, eased her off his lap and stood up.

"We should finish breakfast," he said, regaining some of that cool nonchalance. "I'm sure the food is ice-cold."

Kitty tucked her hair behind her ears. "Okay," she said softly, and took her seat almost meekly.

Her heart was hammering strangely. Some strange energy had been released into the air in those moments of sharing, and she knew, deep down, that nothing would ever be the same again.

# CHAPTER FOURTEEN

"IF YOU COULD have anything, what would it be?" Laurence asked.

Kitty's eyes were closed, and she did not bother opening them. They were out on the deck, under a blazing afternoon sun. Laurence reclined on a deckchair to her left.

They were lazy, slow, languid from the love-making that had lasted most of the afternoon, fragrant with the jasmine and vanilla oil that Laurence was working into her skin with warm, capable hands.

"Kitty?" His voice was low, insistent.

Kitty didn't want to answer. She and Laurence had been at sea for three days—three delightfully hot, seamless, pleasure-soaked days that made the world they'd come from seem a faint and distant memory. They'd eaten and drunk, and bickered and laughed. They'd created their own little world, floating on the blue-gray water. A world where nothing mattered but pleasure, and the odd delight of discovering that they did get along where there were no expectations.

Kitty was also limp with exhaustion, wrung out from being brought to a climax over and over again. Now, as the rays of the sun penetrated her skin, and the faint stickiness of the cocktails they'd had earlier coated her tongue, tart and honey-sweet, she thought hazily that she'd never been so happy. The last time she'd been this happy was when she was a girl who'd thought she'd entered her own Cinderella story—until that life had shattered, and her heart with it.

"Kitty…" His voice rumbled low in his throat, a little impatient. "Roll over."

She didn't want to, and she squeezed her eyes a little tighter. Laurence only used that tone of voice when he wanted to discuss something particularly unpleasant.

His voice took on a crafty lilt. "I need to do your front."

Even the mere suggestion in his voice made Kitty's breath catch in her throat, made her breasts feel heavy and hot. Could it be possible, she thought, to want someone all the time without even a moment to ruminate over how stupid she was being?

Dumbly, she acquiesced, venting breaths on a soundless whimper when his hands skimmed over her ribs, slid upwards to where her nipples already beaded, peaked and aching.

His fingers danced over the tips, then paused. Her eyes flew open.

"Thought that would get your attention," he said dryly.

Kitty glared and slapped his hands away, but with very little conviction, and when he returned them she tried very hard not to squirm.

"If you intend to start something, don't tease me," she gritted out, and his laughter rang out over the deck.

To her surprise, he slid over to her deckchair, hauled her up into his arms, then kissed her till she was breathless and warm. When they surfaced for breath he rested his forehead on hers.

"What would it be?" he asked softly, and shifted, positioning himself between her legs.

She immediately crossed her ankles, pressing them to his back so that the low-slung black trunks he wore abraded against her in a way that was shockingly, incredibly pleasurable.

"None of that," he warned.

She laughed softly, then reached up, touched

his face with the flat of her hand. "There's no way I'm going to answer that question."

"Why not?"

"Because you're going to try and give it to me. And you can't," she said gently.

"I can do anything."

"Not this time."

"Try me."

She smiled, a little wanly. "I made wishes when I was a child, Laurence, but the problem with that is they were ephemeral."

He winced. "That's a little cynical, isn't it?"

She shook her head. "I'm not a cynic. I haven't got the stomach for it. But life has been good enough to me to make me see that dreaming serves no purpose."

Laurence's heavy brows came together; he looked thoughtful. "What was the last thing you wished for, then?"

"Clever man." She shook her head, then decided to keep the tone light. "That you would kiss me. And touch me."

He laughed. "Did you get what you wanted?"

"Yes." She shivered as one long finger traced her collarbone, moved down her chest, alighting on her nipple. "Yes. There," she said, and swallowed hard when his thumb began to circle the puckered swelling bud. Her eyes fluttered shut as waves of pleasure began going through her.

"So sweet," he whispered, and bent his head to capture the tip in his mouth.

There was one gentle scrape of his teeth, and she jumped, but he was holding her fast, and then his mouth was moving lower, growing gentler with each inch of quivering skin.

By the time he'd reached his destination she hardly knew which way was up.

Later, when they'd showered off the oil and had lunch, Laurence asked her to come to his study. It was the only cabin on the ship that stayed locked, and when he pushed open the large double doors with both hands Kitty blinked.

It was as if his Midtown office had been dropped in the center of this floating museum.

Despite herself, she was impressed. The entire east wall was a large, sleek digital screen that stretched from floor to ceiling. Laurence jogged over to it and flipped a switch, and Kitty gasped out loud, pressing her hands to her mouth.

It was a photograph of her from the television interview, larger than life. Laurence had been airbrushed out. The hair, the makeup, the dress—it all worked together to perfectly portray the image of a woman she'd been trying desperately to be for the past several years.

She crept forward, touched the screen with unsteady fingertips. The image dissolved, reverting to a clean, minimalist website.

Laurence came up behind her, pressed a slim remote into her hand. "Take a look," he whispered, and his arms wrapped around her, holding her close. "I thought we could refine it while we're at sea. Together."

Kitty swallowed and did so.

There was a location tab, with photographs of an enormous light-filled office. The address wasn't one she knew, but the location was one of the more fashionable streets in the Financial District. She clicked on another. There was a portal for applications, a donors' page, and another that featured her most recent contributors—including the Muellers.

"When did you have time to do this?" she whispered.

Laurence chuckled low in his throat. "Just keep looking."

The last page was dedicated to her clients, and this was the one that made Kitty's hand fly up, cover her mouth. Three of the young people she was currently helping flashed up in full color, styled impeccably, their smiling teenage faces flanked by concise biographies.

*Proudly supported by Katherine Asare*, they all said.

She felt a lump rise in her throat. "Laurence..."

He released her and stepped back, his eyes bright. "The building is being renovated as we speak, and it will be ready when we disembark," he said briskly. "I know what you want most in life is to help people, so I want to give you that."

*Oh, Laurence.*

Overcome, Kitty stepped back, pressed her hands to her face.

Laurence tugged them away sternly. His own face was pleased, but he spoke briskly to cover it up.

"No time for that," he ordered. "There's a lot of work to do, and if we can do it here it'll be better. I've got a video conference set up with the team I've recruited for you; they'll bring you up to speed. And—"

"Laurence..."

"Desmond wants in as well. He's quite taken by you," Laurence added with some disgust.

*"Laurence."*

He blinked, looked at her and frowned. "What?"

She stood on tiptoe and pressed her lips to his.

"Oh," he said, when she pulled back to breathe.

His face was as she'd never seen it before… soft round the edges and almost tender.

"Kitty—" he began, reaching out to cup her face.

*I can't do this.*

No matter how much she wanted to, she couldn't.

The past three days with Laurence had proved something she'd always known in her heart of hearts: people were more complicated than they seemed, and Laurence was no exception. He was a link to her past, an antagonist, and recently, in the oddest way, a friend and a protector. He'd managed to penetrate the barriers she'd erected *because* of him, and this power left her more frightened than she'd ever been in her life. Not of Laurence, per se, but of herself, and how exposed he'd leave her if she let him in.

*When he's done with you, he'll leave you.*

And when he did, she'd be devastated.

She shook her head and stepped back before he could touch her, before he could say something else that would make this harder, that would crumble her resolve.

"Laurence, this is incredible. But I—" She took a deep breath, balled her hands into fists. *Courage.* "I can't accept it."

He actually reeled. "I'm sorry?"

"I can't accept any of it." She swallowed. "That office alone probably cost—"

"You are not to think about cost!"

Kitty shook her head gently. She could feel her mouth trembling the way it did when she wanted to cry; she hoped she'd be able to keep it together until she could get somewhere relatively private.

"Please," she whispered, and her voice cracked a little. She had never seen him look so absolutely fierce before.

"I don't understand," he said, and his voice was tight. Angry. "We had terms, yes, but that was before we—" Color rushed up to his face.

The air was heavy with unspoken words, and Kitty's heart gave a quick, traitorous beat. Before what? Before they'd had sex? Laurence certainly wasn't in love with her.

"It's my— I have values, Laurence. One of them is simplicity. This is—"

"It's modeled on one of the finest charities in the city," Laurence spat out. His face was stormy.

"I know." She took a deep shuddering breath. "But I don't want to run my foundation like that, Laurence. I've been in the same position as these kids, and I've seen what money can do to help them. But after my experience with your father

I decided I'd only take money from people who had it and give it to people who didn't. I don't want to retain anything for myself, Laurence. I live simply. I use a shared office space—"

"Yes, you seem to enjoy mentioning that." Laurence was speaking through his teeth. "Very noble of you."

Kitty shook her head. "It's not about being noble." *Enough of the meandering. She had to be honest, now.* "I can't take money from you, Laurence."

"But you're all right hanging out on a yacht for three days and crashing parties?"

Kitty felt the blood drain from her face.

*He's hurt*, she told herself, swallowing hard. *Don't take it personally.*

"You brought me here," she said, taking a step back. "And you said this was about contacts, Laurence. I've never asked for anything else."

"What if I want to give you more?"

The words were soft, almost too soft to hear, and fear rushed up, paralyzed Kitty to the spot. She bit back what would have been a soft moan. *No.* Laurence couldn't mean this, not with his iron-clad control and his lack of trust, and she couldn't believe it even if he—

The fear grew inside her, obliterating the thought. *This wasn't real.*

And if she gave in, let him in—

She'd recovered from losing his parents. She knew as much as she knew her own name that she'd never be able to recover from losing him.

"Laurence—"

There was frustration on his face. "I owe you this, at least. And besides that—"

Kitty swallowed once, twice, three times. Her heart was beating so fast she could hear it thrumming, liquid and hot in her ears. The look on Laurence's face…

*Run. Get out. Now.*

She could not allow Laurence to say something he wouldn't be able to take back, or something she wouldn't be able to forget he'd said.

Before he spoke she cut in, panic bleeding into her voice. "Laurence, I want to leave."

"Kitty—"

"No. Now."

Kitty concentrated on her breathing.

*In. Out. In. Out.*

"I'd like you to arrange me transport off the yacht, Laurence. Before nightfall. I can't stay here anymore. I'd like to go home."

* * *

*What?*

Laurence could not comprehend what she'd said—not at first. He simply stared at her, soft and lovely, in a filmy blue dress that blended perfectly into the sky behind them.

He'd picked it himself, after their lovemaking in the pool that morning when he'd caught her, wet and slippery as a mermaid, flush against the mosaic wall, palmed her breasts, her hips, lapped water off her skin and finally, after much wheedling, with her pink tongue darting softly across her lips, let her bend over her lap, take him in her mouth.

It had been as if they were driven by a sort of desperation to consume as much of each other as they could, and his skin still tingled at the thought.

Why the *hell* was he thinking about that *now*?

He worked his tongue round the inside of his mouth; it was dry as ash. He would have to speak, and he could not allow his voice to shake with anger, or with anything else.

There was pain on her beautiful face. "Laurence, please try to understand—"

Her *treacherous* face.

He turned his back, picked up his phone. In

a few clipped words to Cordelia transport was arranged, and he turned back. He saw Kitty's face blanch, and she took a step back. *Good.* He wanted her to feel something as harsh as what was ripping out his insides now, even if it was fear.

"Laurence. Please don't be angry—"

*Angry?* That was an underestimation. He felt bruised inside, as if someone had been trying to claw their way out. He would lash out; he had to.

"You have refused," he said low, "an offer that took a *tremendous* amount of time and preparation—"

"I never asked for that!"

"After draping yourself in silk and letting me have you in every corner of this yacht?" His voice was growing low, malicious, and all too familiar. He'd heard his father use it many times—sometimes with staffers, sometimes with his mother, but mostly with Laurence himself.

Kitty's face had turned ashen, he noted, without much pleasure.

"I cannot believe you'd say something so hateful to me…" she whispered.

He lifted his shoulders. A dark ugliness was taking over his speech, dictating his movements. All he knew was that Kitty was leaving, that she'd bested him, and he must strike back. He stared her down, coldly, till she began to wring her hands and tears slowly made their way down her cheeks. He did not relent. He would not relent.

"Laurence," she said, and she swallowed hard. "Please. It was not my intention to hurt you—"

"Your choices are a matter of *supreme* indifference to me," he said icily. "Good thing we're close to the helipad. Let's get you up there, sweetheart. Now."

"Laurence, my things—"

"I'll have them shipped. Up. *Now.* Chopper will be ready to go in ten minutes, so you'll only have a short wait."

Kitty flinched, but he ignored it. He had to ignore it if he was to hold on to the rage that was the only thing that kept the sick feeling of dread at being left, being *abandoned*, from creeping up in his chest.

After he'd talked to her, opened up about things he'd told no one else, even Desmond… Kitty was the first one he'd trusted to see the truth about him, because on some level he'd thought she'd *seen* him.

If she had, she must not have liked it, because she was doing *this*.

Laurence wrapped a hand round her forearm, tightened it slightly. "I'll carry you up if I have to."

"Laurence—"

"Now!"

A tiny sob broke from her throat but she obeyed—for once—drawing her skirt round those long, slim legs that had been wrapped tightly around him only hours ago. His skin heated at the memory, which made him even angrier.

"Move," he said shortly.

The walk to the helipad was short, and Kitty did not look at him. She might be crying, but he refused to verify it by looking directly at her. When she was gone—when she was out of his line of sight—he would lie down in his dark stateroom and face whatever demons she'd left him.

When they reached the little alcove that served as a waiting room for passengers, she turned a ravaged tear-stained face and tilted it up to his.

"Laurence…" she said.

He did not know what she wanted to say, and did not want to hear it. He shook his head and reached out to place his hands at her waist, lifting her in one smooth motion into the waiting chopper. The pilot was running checks, clearly flustered at the short notice.

Kitty did not settle into her seat; she leaned out through the door instead. "I'm sorry," she said.

There was pity on her face, along with regret, and he could not allow that. He could not let Kitty see how far inside his heart she'd managed to worm herself, or how much all this affected him.

This wasn't just about her turning down his offer. She'd rejected *him*, and whatever had bloomed between them over the past couple of days. He hadn't even had a chance to put a name to it or realized that he wanted to before now.

The chopper's blades stilled while the pilot fiddled with the controls and they were thrown suddenly into an eerie silence. When he spoke, at first his voice seemed much too loud.

"Go," he said, roughly.

Then, he signaled to the pilot and stepped back to safety, both physical and emotional.

The thrumming of the blades drowned out all other sound, and the chopper lifted off into the sky.

## CHAPTER FIFTEEN

WHEN KITTY WAS a child, placed in a particularly bad or lonely home, she'd sometimes cry
till she was sick…until the tears left her with a
headache so violent that she could do little but
lie feebly in her bed and let sleep take her.

She hadn't cried a single tear in those years
between her leaving the Stones and connecting
with Laurence again. Now it was as if a flood-
gate had been unleashed and she cried. First in
the chopper, then in the subway, and now in a
taxicab , where the driver asked her, alarmed, if
anyone had hurt her.

"No, I'm an idiot," she managed from the
depths of her swollen face.

At last, in the safety of her room, she bolted
her door, curled up in a ball on her bed, and
wished quite frankly that she could disappear,
fade away. Nothing had hurt this badly—not for
years. It was the rawness of a heart that had been

injured beyond repair, and the memory of the look on his face.

*You did the right thing*, she told herself. *You did the right thing.*

It was always less painful to give something up rather than have it taken away. She'd been proactive this time.

Then why did it hurt so badly?

Kitty could not trust that whatever had sparked between her and Laurence Stone would have blossomed into anything more than a few idyllic days on the open sea and a return to a full bank account. She did know, however, that she had been losing her heart, and losing it fast—and she'd needed to sever their connection on her terms.

Since that fateful night at the Park Hotel, Laurence had steamrollered his way through her defenses, never giving her more than a cursory listen. But for once she'd escaped having the floor fall out from under her—by ripping it from under him.

Scorched earth. It was the only approach that would work with a man like Laurence. He'd never listen unless you made him...*insufferable* man.

The thought ended on a sob in the back of

her throat. How she missed him already, though it had only been a few hours. Her bed seemed small and cold and inadequate—not because it was humble, but because it was empty, and she was alone.

*Get used to it*, she told herself savagely.

Laurence was never going to be an option, and doing what she had had achieved two goals in one swoop. One, she'd extracted herself from a situation that had grown more dangerous by the day, and two, she'd sent a message to Laurence Stone that he'd never be able to ignore.

*You did the right thing.*

Laurence lingered on the *Triumph* for a full day before he went ashore. He wanted to give Cordelia time to wipe all traces of Kitty Asare from his life.

He signed the Mueller contract the day he arrived, and the only mention of Kitty was from Cordelia.

"It's done," she said, in answer to his questioning look.

She added with a completely blank face that she would see to it that footage of the video that had started all this would be scrubbed from the Internet.

He laughed a bit sardonically and waved her out. He stared at a proposal from the art department for a full half-hour without reading anything, then went into his first official meeting with the Muellers feeling as if he was walking to his execution.

He'd gotten exactly what he wanted—and so had Kitty, in a way. He'd denied her nothing. Yet he was left with a hollow feeling that only increased as the day went on—and for the first time in his life Laurence Stone left work early, waved his car off, and walked.

He couldn't go back to the *Triumph*, where he'd be reminded of that ugly scene…how he'd lashed out at her with his words. Her essence would be everywhere. In the air, in the staterooms where they'd eaten and laughed and made love.

How had she managed to worm her way into his inner sanctum and then, eventually, make a fool out of him? His skin prickled with humiliation as he remembered what he'd done for her and how she'd effectively thrown it back in his face. He who had never made a concentrated effort to go out of his way for anybody…

"Ungrateful," he gritted out through his teeth, and suddenly he wanted nothing more than to find Kitty Asare, make her lift that dimpled chin and look him in the eye and tell him why.

The thought cramped his lungs. He had to stop and take a breath, look around. He was surprised to see how far he was from the office. He reached for his phone, ready to call his car, then left it and continued to walk, thinking harder than he'd ever done in his life.

Before he knew it, he found himself descending into the subway. He hadn't taken it since he was a teen, but he remembered the anonymity of it, the gentle swaying of the cars on the tracks.

Laurence eased himself into one of the grimy orange seats on the Queens-bound F train. He couldn't go to Kitty's—he wasn't even sure how to get to her place from here, and he was one hundred percent certain he'd never pursue her again. But there was something soothing about being underground, where no one knew him.

If he'd been one of the hundreds of thousands who rode this system every day, unencumbered by wealth, privilege, and a past that had snatched away all that was good, perhaps he'd have had a chance.

*A chance to do what, Laurence?*

The thought that perhaps he'd wanted a chance with Kitty Asare made him lift a hand to his throat, loosen his collar. He coughed hard, raked his fingers agitatedly through his hair.

*Get a hold of yourself,* he told himself sternly. *This isn't you.*

He hadn't been himself since the Park Hotel, what seemed a lifetime ago. And he wasn't sure he could find his way back to the man that person had been, or even if he wanted to.

When Laurence emerged in a part of Queens he didn't recognize, he eased himself onto a park bench, grimaced at what he was sure was years of grime, turned on his mobile, and dialed. His personal mobile, this time.

"Hello?"

"Aurelia," Laurence said dryly. He must be feeling better, he thought, feeling a hint of a smile take over his face, if the shock in his former companion's voice gave him so much pleasure. "Are you still in Dubai?"

"I'm not." Her voice was wary. "I'm back in New York. And I'm practically engaged," she added warningly.

"Don't worry, this is not a social call," Laurence said sarcastically. Then he remembered that he wanted to talk to her, and sarcasm probably wasn't the best way to start the conversation. Desmond would have been the most natural candidate for this, but Desmond wasn't a woman.

He hesitated, wondering how best to—

"How have you been, Laurence?"

Unwittingly, Aurelia gave him an opening.

"I see that you replaced me without much effort, with an absolutely tearing beauty. Who is she?"

That was all it took, and the story spilled out— an abbreviated version, anyway. The party, the proposal, Kitty's defection from the *Triumph*.

Aurelia was quiet at first. "Why are you telling me this?" she said finally.

Laurence exhaled noisily. "You're a *woman*. I need to know what you think."

He could practically feel Aurelia roll her eyes. "I think you need therapy."

"Aurelia," Laurence said, "this never happened with you. I just need an outsider's opinion."

Aurelia had known his parents, known him since childhood.

She was silent for a moment, and when she did speak her voice was grave. "I don't know," she said. "But don't go after her, Laurence. Not yet. Even if you are serious."

"Why?"

"I mean it. Let her reach out first." Aurelia paused. "She's proud, and you're overbearing." She stopped again, as if considering. "And self-centered. And arrogant. And pushy—"

"Okay, your point is made," Laurence said irritably.

"What I mean to say is you'll never know if she's in it because she wants to be or because you talked her into it, ad man."

Laurence compressed his lips.

"Sometimes I wonder if you can differentiate between what's real and what you've made up, and that can be pretty jarring for a woman. Let her know you're there, and then leave it alone." Aurelia paused. "She's had the rug yanked out from under her so many times it's ridiculous. If you want her, Laurence, you're going to have to make her believe that you're not going to abandon her. But to do that you also have to decide whether or not you want her to stay. *Do* you?"

For the first time in the conversation Laurence had no words, and after a long moment Aurelia laughed, soft and incredulous.

"My God, you really are in love, aren't you?"

"Aurelia—" He was *not*. He couldn't be. But

he could not deny it out loud, and his face was hotter than it had ever been in his life.

"Listen… You don't have to take my advice," Aurelia said dryly. "Just know that if *I* were ever dumb enough to fall in love with you I'd want to be holding the controls."

# CHAPTER SIXTEEN

KITTY HAD BEEN determined to escape her entanglement with Laurence with both her heart and her head intact—and she managed to do so for the most part. It had been a clean break. Everything, even down to the dress she'd been wearing the night she'd fled the *Triumph*, had been inventoried and given back to Cordelia. Every penny had been accounted for, and Kitty was left with the satisfaction of knowing that Laurence would never be able to take anything back because she hadn't allowed him to give her anything.

What Kitty couldn't shake, though, was the look on Laurence's face when she'd told him she was leaving. He'd looked…gutted. Betrayed. For the first time since she'd known him he'd looked as if he gave a damn about something.

*Men like him don't need anybody*, she told herself sternly.

Still, she couldn't get his face out of her mind. The events of the past several weeks began playing in her head like a montage from a film, but they didn't concentrate on events as much as they did on the look on his face in certain moments. There had been that veiled interest the night he'd taken her to his suite, and she'd given in to impulse and kissed him. There had been amusement whenever she was angry, even more so when she flew into a rage. There had been a curious softness those one or two times when she was sad, an intensity that had burned through every part of her body when they made love…

The fact that she was even thinking of any of her sexual encounters with Laurence Stone as *making love* was terrifying in and of itself.

Still, there was something else that had sparked between them—something deeper, something both beautiful and heartbreaking. It had surfaced that last heated time they'd spoken…something she was terrified to seek a name for.

Why had Laurence done that for her?

More than that, why did she care so much?

Kitty's head ached.

She remembered who she had been, and who Laurence had been, and who they were now.

She dared not think about who they could have been…

\* \* \*

Kitty launched her newly revitalized, expanded foundation on the last day of summer, when the hot, sticky days New Yorkers had been enduring for months had faded to something gentler, softer round the edges, balmier.

May, when she'd last seen Laurence, seemed years ago, but his imprint on her heart felt as fresh as ever. Perhaps, she thought, and swallowed hard. Perhaps *this* would finally be what eradicated him from her mind.

She'd chosen to have the party, after some consideration, at one of the many estates on Long Island out in the Hamptons that overlooked the water. Yes, it was a foundation for young people from the city—but it was a fundraiser, too. And after working with Laurence & Haddad, even for a short period of time, she'd picked up a thing or two about creating a fairy-tale facade to encourage people with too much money and too little imagination to buy into the fantasy. She'd even reached out to Cordelia, asking her for advice on a venue.

The woman had sounded surprised to hear from her, then cautiously pleased. "I'd suggest Long Island. The Hamptons," she'd said briskly, after sentiment had been done away with. "There's some lovely houses out there… very uncommon styles for New York, almost a West Coast look. I'll send you an agent."

She had, and the man had got back to her after a week with the perfect place—a large villa of white stone close to the beach, well within her price range. The owner, she'd been told, lived in the city and had only recently purchased it, so she'd be welcome to go the night before, give herself a little vacation.

Kitty had welcomed the opportunity. For the first time since she'd graduated she would allow herself time to rest, to enjoy herself. Work had been steady and had kept her incredibly busy. She'd had little time to think about Laurence Stone, though he occupied her thoughts during nearly every waking moment.

In an impulsive moment she knew she'd likely regret, Kitty had sent him an invitation—Cordelia and Desmond, too. The latter two had responded with enthusiasm and written generous checks, but she'd heard nothing from Laurence.

She'd grown so busy as the date approached that she forgot to be disappointed some days— except, she told herself sternly, what was she disappointed about? *She* had left *him*…deserted whatever had been budding between them. Perhaps there were some questions that simply would never be answered.

The day before the launch Kitty left for the Hamptons early, renting a car and driving out. She picked up her small, nervous, chain-smoking events manager at the train station, and they drove east together.

The two of them eventually reached a charming villa situated at the end of a shady street. It was completely ensconced in a flower garden and the vivid blooms, even this late in summer, nearly obscured the house, their heady scent filling the air. A mosaic garden path led to a door of smooth wood so silken the grain could not be felt. Beautiful figures were carved on it in relief.

Kitty focused on them before the events manager fumbled at the door, then pushed it open and handed Kitty a key. The villa was enormous, clearly ready for her vacation. Floor-to-ceiling windows were bolted tightly but would, she knew, let in sea breezes during the day, filling the villa with the scent of the ocean.

"Dining room is there," he said, pointing vaguely to the right. "Pool there. Stairs to roof there. I'll see you at eight." Yawning, he touched his cap and headed off.

Kitty was glad she'd come early; it would be

heaven to spend some time at rest in this beautiful place. She'd soak in the tub, read a good book, take a long walk on the grounds before the caterers and decorators arrived in the morning. She took a moment to look around, straightening up in pride. *She'd* done this. By herself, with no help from anyone, and she was glad for it.

She stripped off her clothes methodically, had a long bath, then donned a filmy white nightdress that she'd bought on a whim because it was pretty. When the doorbell rang as she prepared a cup of tea she thought nothing of it. Perhaps it was the party planner, or maybe it was her host, bringing towels or milk or some other little luxury from his own estate miles away.

Anyway, this was the Hamptons, not Queens, she thought as she threw open the front door.

Her cry was muffled by Laurence Stone who, when he saw her, immediately reached out and pulled her into his arms.

"Don't scream," he said, but of course she did.

## CHAPTER SEVENTEEN

"You," Kitty said, once they were inside the entryway and the door was bolted against the night, "are trespassing!"

"Kitty—"

"You're also unbelievable."

If Kitty kept talking, and at this speed, perhaps her heart would descend back into her chest cavity, where it belonged. She hadn't seen him in months, but her body, apparently, remembered precisely what her mind had tried to forget.

"I should have known when I sent you the invitation that you'd try something like this."

"I didn't—"

"The night before the launch, too," she said. "I knew you were outrageous, Laurence, but this—"

"Kitty."

"You didn't even have the courtesy to—"

"Kitty!"

She paused. There was absolutely nothing Laurence could say that would make her think he hadn't somehow planned to ruin this for her.

*"Kitty."*

She lifted her chin in her old gesture, forced herself to listen. "What?"

"Truly, I didn't know you were here until tonight." His mouth twitched, just a little. "And I'm not trespassing. I own the house."

*I own the—*

Kitty stared at him dumbly. "You don't own a house."

"I didn't. Not until a few weeks ago." Laurence rubbed a hand on his head a little sheepishly. "A girl I like told me it was stupid for me not to own one, so I went looking. I put it up to rent for events since…" He trailed off. "Since I'm not quite ready to move in yet."

*Oh.*

Kitty groped for the nearest chair and sank down into it. She couldn't imagine what her face must look like.

Laurence looked at her keenly for a moment, then eased into a chair of his own. "I presume you didn't know who the owner was," he said. "I also presume Cordelia suggested the place?"

"You bought a *house*?"

"I bought a house. I wasn't even going to open

your invitation, but I did tonight. When I saw the address…" He trailed off. "Cordelia didn't even bother trying to hide what she did."

Kitty pressed her hands to her face. Laurence was looking at her intently, as if searching for something. He must not have found it, because he leaned back, his handsome face closing off.

"I'll leave you, then," he said. "You have my word…just think of me as the landlord. I won't show up tomorrow."

"Laurence…" said Kitty, softly.

"I didn't tell you all that rigmarole so you could give me Bambi eyes," Laurence said, sounding like his old self. "I am *fine*—"

"You bought a *house*…" Kitty said in wonder.

"Yes, we've covered that, and— What are you doing?"

Kitty was crossing the space between them, light-footed, with a look in her eyes that he'd never seen before without a veil of uncertainty over it.

She dropped clean into his lap with very little grace.

He grunted in surprise, but had no time to recover. Her long arms were looped round his neck and his senses were overwhelmed by everything he'd already grown to love about her body. Soft, yielding flesh. Warmth. The headiness of oil and the sweetness of powder. She pressed her warm cheek to his, and then her lips were at his ear. They were trembling, as was her body.

"I've missed you," she whispered. "You came." *She'd missed him.*

"Well…" Laurence said. He was uncomfortably aware, once again, of her closeness, as well as of the warmth filling his chest so full he thought it might burst. "All right…"

An absolutely feral smile crept over Kitty's face. "You're blushing," she accused.

Damn his complexion. He chose to answer that by shooting her one of his famously hard looks, but she looked as amused as Desmond was prone to do, and reached out, cupped his face in her hands.

Her tenderness stole his breath. Slowly, deliberately, he palmed her thighs.

Kitty's breath hitched. "Laurence—"

It would be so easy to lift the barrier of her skirt, to relieve the need already surging through him, but Laurence didn't want to do that. This would be the scariest thing he'd ever done in his life—akin to throwing himself off a cliff— but he had to offer this to Kitty as a gift, not a bribe, when there was no expectation of a deal working out.

Laurence hated uncertainties, and the uncertainty of love was something he had not been able to risk—until now, when the alternative, losing Kitty, was simply…

"I love you," he said.

"I love you," he repeated, in a low husk that sounded nothing like she'd heard before.

And some wild, hungry thing inside of Kitty, where she'd kept it for so long, leapt at those three simple words, seized it so tightly she knew it would be impossible to release it.

She tried to speak but emotion tightened her throat. She could cling to him, however, and she did, gripping his muscular forearms so tightly she worried she'd leave a mark. She needn't have worried, though. Laurence was sweeping her up, cradling her so tenderly she felt more secure than she ever had in her life.

"I *love* you," he said a third time, so emphatically that she had to smile. "Okay?"

"I know," she choked out. "Okay?"

Tears were running down her face, but somehow this time she didn't mind.

Laurence whisked them away with his thumbs,

an expression of tenderness on his face. "Are you all right?"

She nodded, unable to speak.

"First woman I've said that to—ever—and she starts crying," he said to no one in particular.

Kitty laughed and hit his chest. "Put me down."

"Never," he said with remarkable gentleness, and he sighed a little, and then he kissed her.

Kitty had never been kissed like that before—not by him nor anyone else. He kissed her as if there were words he wanted to say that had no language except for this. His lips moved warm and slow over hers, not tentative, but savoring, and she knew her body's responding surge wasn't lust, it was desire. A desire to be loved completely, and by this man in particular.

When he finally set her on her feet Kitty was so wobbly she leaned on him, closed her eyes. "I'm not very good at this," she whispered.

There was so much she still wanted to say. She wanted to say that she wanted them to be like this forever, in this cocoon of warmth and love. She wanted to say that she'd missed him so badly in the last few weeks it had become a physical pain. She wanted to say—

"No, you're not," he agreed.

Indignant, Kitty looked up at him, and the

smirk on his face made her huff. She pushed back against his arms, but he held her fast.

"I meant what I said," he said, his eyes bright. "You don't have to say it back…not till you mean it. But I'd like us to— I mean, if you wanted—"

Laurence Stone at a loss for words was something she had never seen before—that was certain. She allowed herself to enjoy it for a fraction of a second before reaching up and lacing his fingers with hers.

"Thank you," he said, almost humbly, then lifted her hand to his lips.

Kitty took a breath. "What happens now?" she asked after a moment.

He leaned forward and rested his head on hers. Contact with him was heaven, and her body already ached, deliciously, in anticipation of the hours ahead of them.

Laurence smiled, just a little. "You could marry me, you know."

Kitty's head jerked up, her eyes flew open wide, and she attempted taking a step back before she could stop herself. "You're not serious—"

The smile widened into laughter. "I'm perfectly serious."

"I— Don't be ridiculous," Kitty faltered, but

there was an odd fluttering in her chest that hadn't been there before.

*Marriage?*

She'd be insane to consider it. But Laurence was turning over her left hand, a determined look in his dark eyes.

She tried to pull away, with little success. "I can't—"

"Not now," he agreed, and slid his arms down to span her waist. "But move in, at least. Test the car before you buy it."

Kitty sighed as her body softened into his; it wasn't even of her own volition anymore. She closed her eyes, rested her head on his broad shoulder. "You're the most absurd person I've ever met in my life," she said, and yelped when his hands slid down to squeeze her bottom.

When she opened her eyes, his were boring into hers. "Kitty," he said, and his voice was soft. "You know how deathly serious I am about my deals. Marriage is a contract, and once I manage to win you in matrimony—no matter how long it takes—you're *mine*. We'll make a home together…" he added.

His eyes looked distant, as if he were seeing something that did not exist yet but was still as real as the feel of his arms round her.

"Maybe here—maybe somewhere else. You'll run your charity and make me repurpose my clothes. And quite possibly, if you hate this place, we'll even live in *Queens*, and we can foster kids of our own…as many as you want—"

"I take offense to the 'even Queens' bit," Kitty said, but she was laughing. Happiness was filling her chest as sunlight would fill a room, warming, melting, and pushing outwards.

*Home.*

The word hit that tender, vulnerable place in the innermost recesses of a heart she hadn't realized was still so soft.

She managed to muster some acid into her voice when she answered, though. Although she suspected by the look in his eyes that he wasn't taking her seriously—not at all.

"I'm not a business deal, Laurence." Trust Laurence Stone to find the most unromantic way possible to propose and still have her considering it. "And I'm not going to marry you," she added. "Not now."

"Not *now*?" he repeated, a gleam appearing in his eyes at the caveat.

She felt herself blush, and ducked to press her face into the crook of his neck. This moment was for drinking him in and wondering how it was possible to want someone so absolutely. She would say she loved him, and soon—the words were already on the tip of her tongue—but in this moment she was overwhelmed.

The thought of being his bride, of belonging to him so completely—

"I can't right now…it's too much," she whispered, and slid her hands beneath his shirt to the hard wall of his chest.

Her body ached for him so badly she could barely speak. His muscles tensed, but he didn't pull away, didn't solidify his control. He let her hands wander, and when they skimmed where he already strained for her he did not redirect them. He took a deep breath instead, smiled a little as he looked down at her face.

"We both have a ways to go," he admitted.

Kitty nodded, tilted her lips up to meet his. They did. But, for the first time in her life, giving herself over to someone felt like a certainty rather than a risk. One day soon she'd be able to say aloud the words that her heart was whispering now.

*I love you.*

# EPILOGUE

"IT GETS BETTER every year," Kitty murmured to her husband, looking out over the party.

The enormous courtyard of Kitty and Laurence's Southampton villa was filled with people—donors, potential donors, and some of the kids that Kitty had helped over the years. A pianist sat at a vintage Steinway, playing jazz tunes, servers circulated with ice-cold champagne, fruit, angel food cake piled high with fresh whipped cream.

One Step Ahead hosted this fete to celebrate its intake of young people each summer, and the event was becoming legendary, drawing donors from near and far who wanted to make a difference. They were expanding. There was talk of a similar program in Ghana, maybe an orphanage, a university...

She and Laurence were foster parents as well: for a year now they'd housed two chubby-cheeked pre-teen girls—sisters who were far more angelic, Laurence said, than he had ever been. Her union with Laurence had taken her vision beyond her wildest dreams, and two wandering spirits had merged to make the perfect home.

*Home.*

Kitty closed her eyes, indulging in a moment against the warmth of her husband's broad chest. She shifted so that she could look up at him and Laurence picked up her left hand, kissing the slim ring of Welsh gold that glowed against the deep tints of her skin.

*I love you.*

Those three elusive words had come out eventually, less than a month after she and Laurence had transitioned from a fake relationship to a real one. She'd whispered them against his mouth after they'd eaten yet another meal at the little Ghanaian restaurant in Hell's Kitchen. They had been huddled together on the sidewalk, kissing softly, and Kitty had been feeling safer in his arms than she ever had anywhere.

Laurence hadn't said much, but his grip had tightened on her, and that night when they'd reached home he had made love to her with so much intensity she'd covered her face, overwhelmed, as waves of pleasure pulled her body tight.

He'd cradled her to his chest, spoken softly against that tender spot on her neck of rings and weddings and honeymoons and future plans. For once Kitty had indulged him rather than arguing back. She'd known it didn't matter what became of the discussions. As long as they were together she would be content.

*Home.*

She had one now, and he did as well. They'd created it together, and it was perfect.

\* \* \* \* \*

# LET'S TALK
## *Romance*

For exclusive extracts, competitions and special offers, find us online:

**f** facebook.com/millsandboon

⊙ @millsandboonuk

🐦 @millsandboon

Or get in touch on 0844 844 1351*

For all the latest titles coming soon, visit millsandboon.co.uk/nextmonth

# Want even more
# ROMANCE?

## Join our bookclub today!

'Mills & Boon books, the perfect way to escape for an hour or so.'

Miss W. Dyer

'Excellent service, promptly delivered and very good subscription choices.'

Miss A. Pearson

'You get fantastic special offers and the chance to get books before they hit the shops'

Mrs V. Hall

**Visit millsandbook.co.uk/Bookclub and save on brand new books.**

## MILLS & BOON